BENEATH A BILLION STARS

JULIE CAROBINI

DOLPHIN GATE BOOKS

Beneath a Billion Stars (Sea Glass Inn, book #4)

Copyright © 2019 Julie Carobini

ALL RIGHTS RESERVED

Dolphin Gate Books

Cover by Roseanna White Designs

This story is a work of fiction. Names, characters, places and events either are products of the author's imagination or are used fictitiously. Any resemblance to any person, living or dead, is entirely coincidental. No part of this publication can be reproduced or transmitted in any form or by any means, electronic or mechanical, without permission in writing from the author.

JULIE CAROBINI writes inspirational beach romances and cozy mysteries … with a twist. *RT Book Reviews* says, "Carobini has a talent for creating characters that come alive." Julie lives in California with her family and loves all things coastal (except sharks). Pick up a free ebook here: www.juliecarobini.com/free-book/

ALSO BY JULIE CAROBINI

Sea Glass Inn Novels
Walking on Sea Glass

Runaway Tide

Windswept

Beneath a Billion Stars

Otter Bay Novels
Sweet Waters

A Shore Thing

Fade to Blue

The Chocolate Series
Chocolate Beach

Truffles by the Sea

Mocha Sunrise

Cottage Grove Mysteries
The Christmas Thief

All Was Calm

The Christmas Heist

CHAPTER 1

Priscilla stood at the edge of the path overlooking the sea and watched Wade Prince try to make up his mind. She had been up since early morning and every inch of her body ached. But Sophia and Christian's big day had arrived and she was not about to miss it.

Wade, however, did not seem quite as committed.

She considered him, his jaw firmly set. "Well, are you going in?"

Wade's chin snapped up as if he'd been confronted by a wild animal. His brows lowered, darkening his eyes. "Pardon?"

She quirked her head to the side and put her hand on her hat so it wouldn't fall off. They were yards from the chapel at Sea Glass Inn and an early spring breeze began to lift the hem of her sundress. "It's going to be a beautiful wedding, Wade."

His frown deepened. "You know me."

"Of course, I do, darling. I'm Priscilla Cornwall. Meg and I have been friends ever since we met unexpectedly in Italy."

Meg, the bride's sister-in-law, was married to Jackson, president of the family-run company that owned the inn.

"Hmm."

"I've been on staff in the spa for several months now ... you know, as a hairstylist?"

He continued to stare at her, his gaze less-than-dawning.

"I have seen the many changes to the inn that you've helped implement, and well, they are just fabulous." Priscilla didn't mention that she had also witnessed one of the happiest moments of Wade's life, nor the eventual, crushing fallout after his uber-romantic plans were dashed.

He nodded, that scowl marring his handsome face.

Too bad.

Priscilla did not let that look bother her, though, because she had seen his smile before, and wow—high wattage, that one. If Wade Prince had not gone into consulting or business management or whatever it was that he did for a living, he could be quite the contender for the silver screen. His fitted white dress shirt, with its French cuffs, hugged a body that had, no doubt, spent ample time at the gym. And with his skin agreeably tanned, the chiseled edges of his face gave him a youthful look, as did the slight wave in his hair, black and salted at the edges like a margarita.

A musical prelude reached her ears. "Oh, they must be starting." Priscilla stepped off the path and onto the soft grass where the pencil-sharp heels of her strappy shoes plunged deep into wet ground. She gasped, falling forward, nothing between her and the earth ... except for Wade.

He caught her mid-fall.

She jerked her head up, her hat slipping backward, her rust-colored hair in disarray—certainly career suicide for a hairdresser.

"So sorry!" Priscilla gripped Wade's upper arm, torn between crying out in pain from the twist of her ankle or commenting on the firm shape of his bicep. The scent of his cologne tickled her nostrils, in a good way, like a potent essential oil she longed to breathe in deeply.

She tried to avoid eye contact, but couldn't.

He frowned, concern showing in his eyes. "Careful there." He helped her stand, his grip steady.

Priscilla continued to hang onto his arm with one hand while settling her floppy hat firmly back onto her head with the other. "Thank you. I can't imagine what I would have done if you hadn't been there." She flashed him a small smile. "You were my knight in shining armor."

Wade stiffened, his smile restrained, those dark brows of his still pushed together. "Yes. Well, perhaps flat shoes would be a better choice next time."

She let go of his arm.

See? Wade Prince was exactly what Priscilla did not need in her life—another grumpy, devastatingly handsome man. She had married one of those, and look where that got her—a broken heart and a nest egg only a fraction of what she had expected at her age. Not that she was old. But maybe if she had paid attention to the signs, she would not have wasted time marrying Leo, which meant he wouldn't have been able to cheat on her while she worked to support them both.

She bit back a sigh and reminded herself to "chin up." Priscilla still could not believe that Leo had left her for Marnie. The woman had been her neighbor. She had given that woman cuttings of her favorite lavender plants ... straight from her garden.

Priscilla shook off her disappointment, reminding herself how far she had come. The sound of the rushing sea just beyond the path soothed her shaky nerves. She ran a hand down her dress, smoothing the wrinkles, and righted her hat once again before zeroing in on the front door of the chapel. She gasped.

Wade turned around and followed her gaze. A small gasp left him too.

Sophia, the bride, stood at the back of the church, steps from the entry doors, looking more radiant than ever. Behind her, Meg fussed with her veil while Sophia's beloved brother, Jackson strode toward them both with a smile that could light a small city.

Priscilla moistened her lips and took one more glance at Wade. "I know she broke your heart."

If looks could crack a stone, Wade's might have made her crumble. But she didn't crumble easily. Had she been bitter when Leo, who had been on disability due to an injury, took up with her neighbor—a woman who had called her friend? For a little while, yes.

But bitterness solved nothing. That, she had learned.

She noted the way Wade swung his gaze away from her, back to Sophia, and then to her again. He turned fully toward her now, his chin dipped, as if she were something of a curiosity to him. "I want nothing but the best for Sophia," he said. "But thank you for your concern."

She shrugged off the edge that had crept into his voice, but before she could respond, another voice split the air between them.

"Priscilla!" Meg waved at her like a mother looking for her young. "Can you help?"

She nodded and assured Meg with a wave back that, yes, she would absolutely help the bride with her veil. A quickening in her chest caught her by surprise. Priscilla hadn't felt needed in a long while—too long. She had lost her purpose after caring for an injured spouse who ultimately cheated on her. She didn't care to have him back, but purpose? Priscilla would not mind finding that again. Not at all.

Priscilla caught Wade's gaze. "Thank you again for catching me. See you inside?"

He pressed his lips together for a moment, as if assessing her. With all the commitment of a toddler under strict orders, he shrugged and said, "I might be there."

∽

MEG HUGGED HER. "You're a life saver, Priscilla. My hair is perfect and Sophia looks like royalty! Thank you so much for getting up early to spoil us."

"It was my pleasure."

"Who knew that our serendipitous meeting in Italy would turn into such a friendship?"

"Divine intervention. That's what I always say."

Together the women stepped back and watched as Jackson offered the crook of his arm to his sister. The smile he gave her faltered, his eyes watering.

Meg pressed a hand to her cheek. "Now I'm going to cry."

Priscilla whipped out a tissue and handed it over. "You go ahead and cry, honey. My purse is full of them for just such an occasion."

The string quartet paused, the anticipation in the air palpable.

Sophia swung a look toward Meg and Priscilla, her smile wide and glowing. "Thank you both so much," she whispered.

Meg blew her a kiss as an usher the size of a linebacker appeared. "Ready to take your seat?"

She nodded. "Yes, absolutely!" Meg turned back and latched onto Priscilla's arm. "Sit up front."

"Oh, no, I couldn't. I'll just find a place in the back."

"I insist! You've ... you've become like another sister to me," Meg said, that hitch in her voice. "Liddy's holding a space for you, right in front of my mother and Jax."

Priscilla smiled at the mention of Meg's newborn son. She guessed that Meg's close friend Liddy would have her young son with her too. "All right."

Quickly, Priscilla made her way to the front of the chapel and found her seat. Liddy leaned toward her and gave her a squeeze. "Hey, gorgeous."

"Hey, yourself."

"There's so much love in this place, I can't stand it. The groom's been pacing like a lion."

Christian, the groom, fidgeted up at the front of the chapel, not in an anxious way, but with a face full of anticipation. He wrote fantasy novels with a touch of romance and had fallen headlong into a happily-ever-after of his own.

When the first few notes of "The Wedding March" began, Priscilla stood and turned, the bride's presence ushering in sighs all around. She had been a bride once, too, and she had meant her vows with all her heart. Unfortunately, the other side of that equation had not. When temptation came calling his name, he grabbed the apple, so to speak.

Priscilla shook off thoughts of the past and reminded herself, for the second time today, to "chin up." She took in the beauty of the bride as she floated toward the front of the chapel like an angel. After the bride met her groom at the altar, Priscilla cast a glance back over her shoulder, across the rows of whitewashed pews behind her. But Wade wasn't anywhere in view.

CHAPTER 2

Wade allowed the wine to take the edge off of an already tense situation. He had a difficult time swallowing, well, all of it.

Laughter rang out and he snapped a look up. The first dances had all been completed and the rest of the visitors had flooded the compact dance floor that the inn had set up on this precipice overlooking the Pacific Ocean. With so many people twirling and sliding out there, calling attention to themselves, he would have a better chance of laying low at his table along the perimeter of the guests.

He took in the vast sky and flickered his gaze at the calm sea. A sigh helped him to release pent-up emotion. William, the man who had built this place, would be pleased at how his inn was being used this day. Admittedly, Wade spent more time here than necessary, but he had a soft spot for the inn. William had been a mentor to him many years before, and when Wade added consulting and marketing to his list of businesses, Riley Holdings was his first client. Since then—

and especially after William's death—Wade had made the inn a priority.

He glanced at William's children, Jackson and Sophia, who were both out on the dance floor, a testament to lives restored.

"She's beautiful, don't you think?" Meg's voice interrupted Wade's musings.

He nodded. "Your sister-in-law makes a beautiful bride. No doubt there."

Meg shook her head. "I wasn't talking about Sophia, although, of course, she is so lovely." She glanced toward a table at the edge of the dance floor. A woman with flowing red hair sat watching the dancing. "I meant Priscilla."

"Your friend who works in the salon."

"Right. You were talking to her before the wedding, right? I thought maybe ..."

He looked at her, his mind blank. "You thought?"

Meg gave him a confident smile. Jackson's wife was the hotel's sales director, and she was good at convincing people of what they needed. Usually.

The tip of her tongue stuck out between her teeth. Another smile. "Maybe you should ask her to dance."

Wade took another sip of his wine and pulled an envelope out of his suit coat pocket and handed it to Meg. "Actually, I'm about to leave as I have another matter to attend to. Will you see that the happy couple receives this?"

Jackson swooped in between them, just as Meg reached for the envelope. "What are you two whispering about over here?"

Meg gave her husband an admonishing scowl. She took the envelope from Wade. "I hope I didn't say anything to drive you away. I just ... well, we all want to see you happy."

"I agree with my wife." Jackson put a hand on Wade's shoulder. "It's incredible that you decided to come today. Meant the world to Sophia. And to me, especially under the circumstances."

Wade leveled a gaze at Jackson. "Circumstances?"

Jackson glanced at the bride and back to Wade. "Not too many men would attend their ex's wedding and wish them well."

Meg nodded solemnly.

Wade waved a hand at them. "Trust me—I don't think of Sophia as my 'ex'. She's your sister and the daughter of a man who I hold in high regard, even these years after his passing." He shook his head. "I apologize if my demeanor has given you the impression that I did not want to be here."

"Completely understood," Jackson said. "I couldn't help but notice how you've stepped up your traveling lately. All I can say is that I'm glad you have your work to keep your mind busy."

Wade smiled his regret. "I don't think you do understand. I am preoccupied with a ... particular business matter this weekend. Again, my apologies."

Trace, the inn's longtime concierge, joined them. She was known for her direct and eccentric ways. "Hey there, Mr. Prince," she said. "Just stopping by to offer my condolences. You gave it your best shot, though, right? That's all you can do."

"Trace!" Meg said.

Trace chuckled, her eyes still on Wade. She leaned forward. "Don't worry. I have your back. In fact, now that I know the type of woman you're after, I'll be sure to alert you when I meet someone like that."

Jackson cleared his throat. "Trace, I'm sure Wade can handle his personal life without your assistance."

Wade stood. While Trace had surprised him, it was Jackson's reaction that brought a smile to his face—and a distraction he needed. "Thank you, everyone. Excellent event, as always."

The convention services manager showed up and touched Jackson's elbow. "Sir? I have a few items I would like to discuss with you. Would now be a good time?"

Jackson nodded.

Wade and Meg watched Jackson walk away from the event with the manager. He was about to turn and say his final goodbye to Meg when he noticed Priscilla moving toward them. She wore a translucent gown that fit her body well, yet moved like angel wings around her.

He turned away.

Truthfully, he had been a little put off by his encounter with Priscilla earlier today. She certainly was a beautiful woman, but something seemed too set up there for his taste. Been there. Done that. In the six months since he had fallen hard so quickly for Sophia—and lost her to another man—Wade had done some soul searching. Had spent time with God and began to see all the ways he had been neglecting his other pursuits.

He had heeded that call, which is one of the reasons that a new, discouraging development had soured his mood so swiftly.

"You made it after all." She approached him, her mouth smiling. She seemed close to laughter and he might have thought it was alcohol had her eyes not been so clear and focused on him. "Such a beautiful wedding. And this band!"

She swept an arm toward the stage from where big band sounds emanated. "Aren't they fabulous?"

"They are indeed."

She took another step toward him, her scent like fresh rain. He darted a look at Meg, sending an SOS her way.

But Meg did not appear to notice. Or she chose not to.

Priscilla reached out a hand to him. "Dance with me?"

He teetered. It would not be polite to turn her down. On the other hand, he had something he must take care of. Besides, if he were to suddenly begin spending time with another woman so closely associated with the inn, the Riley family would think he was preying on their most beautiful people.

He would not have it.

Wade opened his mouth to give Priscilla his regrets when he felt a gentle shove to his back.

"You have all the time in the world to deal with business," Meg said. "But right now is the time for dancing! Get out there."

Priscilla's hand slipped into his, warm and insistent. A Michael Buble-style crooner had just begun singing "Dream a Little Dream of Me."

His hand molded to her waist and he began to relax. She tipped her chin up, eyes sparkling. "As I mentioned when we first spoke, the improvements at the inn are magnificent. And I understand you are responsible for so many of them."

"I wouldn't say that, exactly."

"No? Meg tells me that you lit a fire under Jackson with your unique ideas and gentle persuasion." She appeared to hold back a laugh on those last words.

An honest smile welled up, probably for the first time in days. "Meg flatters me. Jackson has plenty of ideas of his own.

I only provided the outline and financing ideas to get him there."

"And your considerable business experience."

Her expression was open, kind. He had no reason to believe she was employing any kind of flattery herself. "Tell me about you," Wade said, regarding her. "I recall you mentioning something about meeting Meg in Italy."

"You were listening?"

He stilled. "Of course. Did you think I had not heard you?"

Priscilla nudged him along, her mouth smiling, her eyes unwavering. "You seemed very distracted this morning. Not that anyone would blame you for that. I thought, well, I thought it likely that you did not hear one thing I said to you out there on that lawn."

"Is that really what you thought?"

"But you have proved me wrong."

He worked to make his mind catch up with this conversation. "So," he finally said, "it sounds as if you and Meg have been friends for a long while."

"We met at a restaurant in Italy when we were each traveling alone. We kept up a little, and then I came out here last year for a ... change of scenery."

"From?"

"Virginia. I thought it was time to give the west coast a try for a time."

"And how are you liking it here?"

She nodded as she spoke. "It's a step in the right direction. I apologize if that sounds like a cliché."

He smiled at her again. "Not at all."

They moved around the dance floor with a fluidity Wade hadn't expected. Her meeting with Meg intrigued him. If his memory served him, Meg had gone to Italy to escape her feelings for Jackson—or, at least, that's the way Jackson had explained it. Much more had happened during that trip. And here Priscilla was now, living all the way across the country.

His gaze washed over his dance partner, who was looking over his shoulder at someone—or something, her face pensive. "You have an adventurous spirit."

She flicked a look up at him. "Have you ever paddle boarded?"

"Is this in response to my comment about your adventurous spirit?"

She laughed lightly and gestured briefly toward the sea. "I've been watching paddle boarders all afternoon and I think I would like to try it. You?"

"I don't enjoy the thought of being prey."

"Oh, please."

"I prefer my vessels to have sides—even a kayak would be better than a paddle board, in my opinion."

"I assumed that, but I thought I would ask anyway."

"What do you mean you assumed so? Surely I don't look like someone who could not handle a paddle board."

When she did not answer him right away, he leaned in closer, his eyes connecting with hers. "Right?"

She gave him that dazzling smile of hers. "I'm sure you could handle one just fine. You are always so formal, though. Even your summer clothes look impossibly starched."

He sputtered, shrinking back slightly. "I wasn't aware that my wardrobe was being studied. But let me correct a misperception—I have never used starch on my shorts and T-shirts."

"You wear shorts and tees?"

His mouth dropped open. "Come on now."

She laughed again, not an ounce of shame in her expression. She was enjoying this.

He cracked a smile. "I haven't much time for water sports these days, but if I were—"

"If you ... were?"

He tilted his head down closer to her face again, taking in her eyes. He spoke loudly, over the music. "As I was saying, if I were to ... partake, then my vessel of choice would have sides all around and ample room for movement."

"Is that your final say on the matter, Mr. Prince?"

"It is."

She laughed harder than before, truly enjoying this. If he were honest, Wade would admit that he, too, was enjoying the dance and his partner. He hadn't planned on staying much past the first toast, but somehow, this woman whom he had only met—though she seemed to know him—changed all that.

A dark thought hovered over him. Wade tilted his chin. "You said something earlier that I wanted to ask you about."

"Anything."

"What did you mean when you said that you knew that ... well, you believed that Sophia broke my heart?"

"Well, darling, I was there when you proposed."

"You were there?"

Priscilla's bright smile diminished and she searched his face. "We *all* were. And then after she broke it off, while the others were comforting Sophia, I looked for you." She gave him a little shrug. "You had already fled."

Wade allowed Priscilla's words to penetrate his mind. He had not realized that when he proposed, and subsequently had been dumped, that a crew had witnessed both occurrences.

Priscilla watched him, her expression open, her eyes wide, as if anticipating his response. His mind, usually so pinpoint

BENEATH A BILLION STARS

accurate, felt more like it was stuffed with cotton, myriad ideas and thoughts stuck inside.

Wade's jaw tensed. He should not have come. Should have given his regrets and tended to the other issues that drew at him today. If he had, he might have made some progress there—and he certainly would not be caught in this situation now.

He listened for a break in the music, a point when he could tactfully extricate himself from the dance floor. But another song had already started.

Priscilla intrigued him, but in the few minutes they had spent together on this dance floor, she had managed to twist a key and unlock a part of him that he would rather keep shut. Wade had already blown it twice when it came to romantic entanglements and he wasn't a third-times-a-charm kind of guy.

It was only a dance, he reminded himself. He wasn't looking for anything more. Thankfully so. As his assistant, Laura, constantly reminded him, his calendar was packed. He would not have time for love if it commandeered his Outlook calendar and penciled itself in.

Before the music ended, Wade bowed, uttered a hasty "thank you," and stepped off the dance floor, hoping Priscilla understood.

~

PRISCILLA WATCHED Wade walk off the dance floor and out of view. He didn't look back.

The band continued playing as if nothing had occurred, as if she hadn't just been unceremoniously dumped on the dance floor.

Meg showed up, standing where Wade had stood, her arms

in the two and nine positions. "Hey, babe. Wanna dance with me?"

Thankfully, the ballad ended.

Meg laughed. She dropped her arms. "You planned that."

"Hardly!" Priscilla shouted, not allowing the smile on her face to falter. Why would it anyway? They had simply been dancing. Never meant to be anything more than just that—despite Meg's sudden need to rescue her.

She loved her friend for that.

The drummer cued the band and they began to play "A Hard Day's Night." Partner or not, Priscilla began to dance, fast this time, until a sheen of perspiration made her arms glow.

Meg grabbed her hands and did a little swing around thing, like they were middle school girls on the dance floor.

"Sorry Wade left you stranded," Meg said, rolling her eyes. That reminded her of middle school too.

"I think I went too far," Priscilla shouted back.

Meg shook her head. "He's just having a hard time today. It's not you."

"I told him that I was there when he proposed to Sophia."

Meg gave her a surprised laugh. "You did?"

Priscilla twisted her lips into a rueful smile. She leaned in. "Did I ever tell you about Leo's new beloved?"

Meg winced at the mention of Priscilla's ex-husband's name. "Don't call Leo's other woman that."

Priscilla batted the air as if it were no longer a big deal to her. "Anyway, she used to follow me around, even after he had left me for her."

"Wait. She did? I don't think you've ever told me that."

"It's true. Marnie—that's his new wife's name—was our neighbor and my friend. I used to give her clippings from my garden and we'd sit outside and drink tea and talk about our hopes, our dreams. She wanted to travel the world. Anyway, once they were married she kept contacting me, even going so far as to make an appointment with me at my salon."

"No way."

Priscilla kept her smile as bright as possible. "She seemed to think that I could easily look past husband stealing." She looked away for a moment, a couple of paddle boarders drawing her attention as they rode the surf.

"Are you okay?"

She blinked several times. "Yes, yes. I'm fine. Anyway, this has been a beautiful wedding. I'm only sorry it conjured up things from the past. Not sure why."

"Completely understandable."

Priscilla quirked her chin to the side. "You know that 'seventy-seven times seven' thing in the Bible?"

"The one about forgiving someone that many times?"

"Yes. Well, the thing is—it might have been easier to follow through with that if getting a divorce wasn't as easy as picking up a drive-through latte!"

"I'm sorry."

Priscilla slowed considerably, along with the music. She set her gaze at the sea again. "Perhaps mentioning Wade's old wound to him wasn't quite the best idea."

Meg gave her a sympathetic look. "Oh, I don't know. He's obviously over her or he wouldn't have come to the wedding. At least, he ought to be over her by now."

"Maybe."

Meg put her arm around Pricilla. "If anyone would know about broken hearts, it's you. You've been able to move on after your husband's rejection."

Priscilla raised both eyebrows. "Thank you for putting it that way."

"I'm sorry. You know what I mean."

"In other words, *c'est la vie*. Am I right?"

"There's the woman I met in Cinque Terre," Meg said with a laugh. Another song started, but the sound had been turned down a few levels. Meg flicked her chin toward the three-tiered cake. The bride and groom were approaching it now. "Cake?" she said.

Pricilla grinned. "You don't have to ask me twice."

The sun hovered over the water like a decadent morsel. Priscilla and Meg stepped to the edge of the path, out of the way of the photographer, the waitstaff ready to pounce once the formality of hand feeding cake to each other had been completed. Small children watched the entire event with hungry eyes.

Meg signaled to Jackson, who seemed to be walking aimlessly with Jax in his arms.

When he approached, Meg held out her arms. "I'll take him."

Jackson cooed at his son, who was now safely tucked into his mother's arms. He glanced at them both. "I had to hold Jax back. He wanted to join you on the dance floor, but I convinced him to let you have some girl time out there."

"Yeah, right," Meg said. "You didn't want to dance, so you were grateful to have this little guy as an excuse."

Jackson kissed her temple. "Guilty." One of the staff called his name. He turned back to Meg before leaving. "Tell Priscilla about the press trip."

When he'd gone, Meg bit her lip, a guilty smile on her face. "With everything else going on, namely this wedding, I completely forgot to tell you about a press trip that we've pulled together quite quickly."

"What kind of press trip?"

"We've booked a cruise out to the islands and have invited travel writers from all over the state to join us." She eyed Priscilla. "Actually, it was one of Wade's ideas. He lobbed it toward me in passing one day and I ran with it. He's got a million ideas, really."

"Buying the press? Is that like fake news?"

"Ouch. You wound me."

"Kidding, of course. It sounds wonderful."

"It's going to be. This isn't just for our inn—that would be a little self-serving. Actually, I pitched the idea to the visitors bureau and they, along with several other hotels, are all on board."

Priscilla raised one brow. "No pun intended."

Meg laughed. "Chef will provide box lunches and we'll give the press a complete tour of the waters between here and the islands. Then take a spin around Anacapa Island. They won't have to lift a finger."

"Wow. You really have thought of everything. I'm impressed, Meg." Priscilla sighed.

"What?"

"I was just wondering if you'll see any mermaids while you're out there." She gave Meg a deadpan look. "Or mermen, for that matter."

Meg rubbed her lips together, her brown eyes staring at Priscilla.

"Did I say something wrong?"

"No, not at all. It's just, well, I need a favor," Meg said. "Would you ... would you be interested in taking my place on the cruise?"

Priscilla straightened, confused.

Jax fussed and Meg began bouncing him, her forehead bunched. She looked straight at Priscilla. "I have a confession. It seems that I haven't quite gotten my sea legs after giving birth."

Priscilla gasped. "What? I don't understand."

"Apparently, seasickness in women who have recently given birth is a thing." She sighed, her gaze traveling out toward inky blue sea. "I hopped aboard a simple harbor cruise last week and, well, lost my lunch. I was mortified."

Priscilla reached forward and rubbed Meg's back. "Oh, honey. I'm so sorry! How awful for you."

"I could take something, of course, but I'm still nursing this little guy ..."

"And you wouldn't want to pass motion sickness medicine on to him. Oh, I understand."

Meg peered around, lowering her voice. "There are others I could ask, but you have become such a great encourager to me and a cheerleader for the inn, so I hoped you wouldn't mind stepping in and representing us."

Priscilla thought about that. She loved being a hairstylist and had embraced her new role at the inn, but adventure nipped at her heels. There was no reason she couldn't switch roles for a day, especially to help a friend. "Why not? I'm sure Manuel and Katrina can handle the salon."

"There is one thing, though," Meg said. "And please don't think this is any kind of weird set up—it's truly coincidental. Wade will be there too."

"Oh."

"Don't worry—he'll be with a client, so you won't even have to talk to him. Besides, we already have a full roster so you'll have plenty of other people to talk to and encourage to visit the inn."

Priscilla nodded. "I'll be fine. And I'm happy to help out the inn. Always."

Meg hugged her, snuggling Jax between them. "You're the best. Thank you so much!"

After Meg had gone, Priscilla drifted away from the dance floor and onto the path where she could stand and watch the sunset. Several boats were rolling in, signaling the ending of a day on the water. A tiny rush of excitement met her as she watched them bob along, as if no other care in the world.

That rush tempered some as she thought about Wade Prince. Something about him drew her and had since the moment she watched him propose to the beautiful Sophia. And when she broke his heart? Priscilla felt another overwhelming emotion for him: compassion.

A tinge of regret moored itself to her heart. Priscilla hoped that Wade had not mistaken her attention for anything more than the compassion she'd had for him since she stepped into his story at Sea Glass Inn. She, too, knew what it was like to be hurt by someone she loved, and in her case, by someone who had made a vow to love her forever—only to change his mind and break that vow.

As the glowing orb sizzled into the sea, Priscilla promised herself to never, ever allow that to happen to her again.

CHAPTER 3

She wanted to cry.

A sharp wedge of tears pressed against the base of Priscilla's neck. Another dolphin broke the surface of the water and the crowd of seagoers roared again. Four more dolphins leaped out of the water and back in again, their outer layers in shade of gray and black shiny and glistening. Flags whipped in the wind as Priscilla stood gripping the deck rail, unable to take her eyes from such elegant, yet playful creatures.

A tear dripped down the side of her cheek.

A man with a full head of hair peeking out beneath a baseball cap stood next to her. He, too, stared out to sea. "Magnificent beings, aren't they?"

She wiped away her tear and smiled. "Yes, they truly are. I'm overwhelmed."

He smiled at her. "I can see that."

The voice of their captain spoke through a loudspeaker. "Everyone look toward the stern. They are really putting on a show now!"

Sure enough, dozens of dolphins arced and dove through air and water, over and over again. She crossed her arms on the top of the railing and leaned against them, unable to stop smiling. Despite the floppy hat tied beneath her chin, sea spray misted her skin and deposited salt on her lips.

LeeAnne from the visitors bureau joined her at the rail. She was curvy in pink athleisure, and her feet were shod with Adidas. She leaned toward Pricilla, her voice as low as possible, yet loud enough to be heard above the rippling wind and churning waves. "Meg hit this one out of the park again. You'll let her know, won't you?"

"Thank you for saying so," Pricilla said. "I'm sure she'll be pleased to hear that, especially from you."

"You're quite welcome." LeeAnne continued to stand next to Priscilla, a Cheshire-cat grin on her face. "So, what do you know about the salt-and-pepper hottie at three o'clock?"

Dutifully, Priscilla glanced over her shoulder. Wade was standing next to a stocky man, a real estate investor she had heard would be here. As if to prove her wrong about his uptight wardrobe, Wade wore blue drawstring shorts, a white tee, and slip-on boat shoes. She wondered if he would thank her later …

"So?" LeeAnne interrupted. "Is he single?"

Priscilla's concentration broke. "Excuse me?"

LeeAnne nodded toward Wade. "You know him, right?"

"Ah, yes. Mr. Prince is a lovely man."

"And?"

Priscilla shrugged. "I don't have any insight into his love life. Sorry."

LeeAnne licked her lips and cast a furtive glance toward Wade and his investor friend. "No matter. I'll go on over and introduce myself."

She watched LeeAnne saunter over to the men, clipboard in hand, expectancy on her face. Another whoop went out from the crowd and Priscilla flicked her gaze toward the sea again, with its blues and greens and saturation of wildlife. She inhaled and let her breath out, thankful for the opportunity to experience all of it.

For the next hour, Priscilla did what she came to do: She sang the praises of Sea Glass Inn to everyone she encountered. As their excursion took them out and around Anacapa Island, one of a string of islands off of the coast, she wandered around the deck of the boat, making conversation. She offered hellos and information, and occasionally snapped a photo of newly made friendships.

They were on their way back toward the mainland when Wade showed up at the railing next to her. "You've been busy," he said.

She nodded, her eyes on the sea. "I did what I came here to do—and then some."

"If the hairstylist career becomes tiring, you might want to take up sales and marketing. You're good at it."

"Thank you—hold on a second!" A young boy had darted for Priscilla, his skin as green as a pickle. He held one hand over his mouth and looked at her in horror. "I've got you," she said assuringly, and quickly lifted him high enough to puke over the rail without falling in.

When he was finished, she set him back down on the deck and patted his head. "Feel better?"

He nodded vigorously and ran back to the adults who were sitting on a bench in the center of the deck, none the wiser.

Wade wore a comical smile. "Where did you learn to do that?"

Priscilla waved him off. "That was instinct."

"Then I'm impressed with your instincts."

She smiled. "You would have done the same."

"Doubtful. If the child had run up to me, I would have stood by while he vomited on my shoes."

"Well, now," she said, her voice teasing, "maybe I should have let you step in. Ba dum bump."

Wade held up his hands in surrender, laughter lighting his face. "Okay. All right. You obviously carry the mothering gene."

She smiled at him, but had nothing to add. So she glanced toward the harbor mouth, where they were headed. A paddle boarder rode a shallow wake behind a boat that had slowed its pace after passing a sign on a buoy warning sailors of the harbor speed limit. Her mind went back to the early days with her husband, Leo.

"LET'S HAVE A BABY," she said one Saturday after she'd put away lunch leftovers and loaded the dishwasher.

Leo's right brow shot up toward the ceiling. He lurched forward, onto his feet, wrapped his arms around her waist, and pulled her down onto the overstuffed couch with him.

He grinned, his skin unshaven. "Why would I need a baby when I've already got one?"

Priscilla ran a finger along his grizzled cheek. "I'm serious."

He grabbed her hand and kissed her fingers. "I thought I was enough for you."

"Of course, you are. A baby would enhance what we already have."

Leo sighed. He held her in one arm while reaching for the remote in the other. "What we have is perfect already. Why mess with perfection?" Then he switched on their smart TV.

Priscilla lolled a look at the screen over their fireplace. It was early afternoon, which meant the game was about to start. She snuggled in closer to Leo, whose touch on her waist had loosened some.

"I agree that this is perfect, but I want you to think about it. Will you do that? For me?"

He forced his gaze away from the television and found her eyes. In them she saw uncertainty, but he relented. "Sure, baby. I'll think about it." He kissed her cheek. "Are we good?"

Before she could answer, he'd already turned his attention to football.

"WHAT DO YOU PREFER, Italy or California?"

Priscilla's mind returned to the present. She blinked and took in Wade's expression. He had just asked her a question. "Excuse me?" she said. "I'm sorry. I didn't get that."

His laughter rolled out comfortably. "It was a rhetorical question, really. You mentioned your trip to Italy, where you met Meg. And I asked which you prefer—Italy or California?"

Priscilla flashed back on her meeting with Meg at the top of a steep hill. What a gorgeous day it had been. She had climbed all those stairs, hoping to sweat out her pain. And then she'd met Meg, who was dealing with her own kind of discomfort.

She nodded, remembering. "It was kismet, meeting Meg out there. Brought me here to California, well, eventually it did. And I'm quite content here in my new surroundings." She inhaled more sea air and looked at Wade. "Because of that, it's very difficult to choose one over the other—though I know you probably thought I'd say Italy."

He shrugged good-naturedly. "That sounds fair."

The man Wade had been talking to earlier joined them.

"Priscilla, I'd like you to meet Samuel Facet," Wade said. "Sam, Priscilla is a friend from Sea Glass Inn, a marvelous property and one of today's hosts."

Samuel shook her hand then turned to Wade. "I'll be disembarking the moment we reach the dock. But I'd like to speak to you more about EduCenter and the predicament you're in over there. A mighty worthwhile endeavor. I'm not sure if I can help, but we'll see."

Wade thanked him and they watched as the man made his way through the crowd toward the exit where he would have to wait until they were safely moored.

"EduCenter? What is that?" she asked.

Wade flicked a glance her way, his expression a mask. She did notice, however, a dip of concern hovering above his eyes, his brows lowering. "Listen, about that. I wonder if you could pretend you did not hear any mention of it."

She turned fully to him now, her eyes questioning.

"It's a charity for teens in need, most who are in foster care. We're giving them practical, financial education. It's not math—"

"Which they likely would hate."

"Precisely. I try to teach them ... *we* teach them about finances in the real world. Some kids are falling asleep in Algebra, so we give them tools that excite them. Or try to, at least."

"So ... you're a teacher too?"

His chin dipped and he flashed a look up through guarded

eyes. "It's new for me, but yes, this is something I am passionate about."

"And if you're passionate about it, and you know your stuff—which you clearly do—then you are qualified to teach."

"I try. One thing we also do is make sure the kids have access to full meals when they're on-site. Helps them stay awake."

"Kind of like the two-handed Bible—teach them the word *and* meet their physical need. That's really beautiful, Wade."

"Thank you." He rubbed his lips together, silently watching her before saying, "Don't take this the wrong way, but I'd like to ask that you not share what I've told you with anyone else. I prefer to be as anonymous as possible regarding the center."

"Oh I can't imagine why. It's a worthwhile mission, so why not shout it from the balcony?"

He frowned. "I suppose I didn't phrase it well. It would be perfectly fine mentioning the center as a worthwhile organization with a mission to help children. But I don't care to draw attention to myself in any way."

"I see."

"So we'll keep this between us, at least for now? I only mentioned the situation to Sam because he was a past supporter and had asked for an update."

Priscilla continued to eye him. She turned her back on the sea and leaned against the railing as the chartered boat rolled closer to the landing dock, connecting her gaze with his. "On one condition."

"Of course. What is it?"

She crossed her arms. "I would love to see the center. Maybe I can help. Will you take me there?"

Wade hesitated, his mouth unreadable, his eyes showing a

hint of a surprised smile. "If that's what you want, then of course, I will take you to the center sometime soon."

∾

"Soon" came along faster than he had expected.

For nearly an hour, Wade and Priscilla had been on the road from the coast to a small inland town off the I-5. He pulled his BMW into a parking space at the center and attempted to walk around the car to open Priscilla's door, but she had already exited. She had a look of anticipation on her face and a bag full of who-knew-what on her shoulder as she waited for him to lead the way.

"The entrance is over here," he said.

She followed him into the building, past the lobby where he said a quick hello to Mandy, the receptionist, introduced Priscilla, and then continued down the hall. They reached an open door that said *Director* and stepped inside.

Empty.

Wade turned around. "I was going to introduce you to Candace, our director, but she must be working with the kids right now. Would you like a tour?"

"Please."

They wandered down the first corridor and peeked into a youth room filled with tables and desk chairs, the kind that might be found in a plush office. The whiteboard had a handwritten table with columns of words at the top, such as cellphone, gaming, car expenses, and food.

Priscilla looked up at him. "Part of your Money Smarts course for teens, I take it?"

He grinned. "Something like that."

"Oh good, you're here." Wade turned to find Candace marching up to them, her sleek ponytail bobbing to the beat.

"Hi, Candace. I'd like you to meet my friend, Priscilla. She asked to see the center."

"A pleasure," Candace said, offering a hand. Then she turned her attention back to him. "Wade? I wonder if I could speak to you in my office for a moment?" She didn't add "privately," but it was understood.

Thankfully, Priscilla appeared to understand and not take offense. She touched the crook of his arm. "I'll be fine on my own. Am I okay to wander?"

After she had gone, he ducked inside Candace's office.

The director whirled around to face him, her fist stuck hard into her waist. "They really are pulling funding."

"You're sure."

She turned up a palm, her expression exasperated but resolved. Her brows reached higher than anyone's he had ever seen. "That's what Rosario told me on the phone today. She said that their bottom line was down, so they were making cuts. And we, apparently, are the first to go."

Wade pressed his lips together. He understood the ups and downs of bottom lines. His father had gained and lost so many that those wins and losses had shaped him—and scared him. This was different, though. What he found hard to understand was the reneging of a promise. It ate at him.

He snapped a look at Candace who looked as if she had no hope. Her downcast eyes and frown brought him to his senses. "You do not have to worry about this, Candace. I will take care of everything."

"But ... but our budget depends on these promised funds. The rest of the board has already told me they have nothing to contribute." She exhaled and looked around before looking back to him. She stepped closer and lifted her chin. "What will we do?"

A beat of silence fell between them and he began to pace. After a silent minute had passed, Wade walked toward the exit and stopped. With one hand on the door, he turned to Candace. "Go home and pour yourself a glass of wine and don't worry. I have a plan and will call you tomorrow with details."

CHAPTER 4

A strange kind of peace filtered through Priscilla as she moseyed down the hall, peeking inside various rooms. This center was more like a big, comfortable home made for a family with many children. Unlike the classroom she first poked her head inside, the other rooms were outfitted with couches and throw rugs, recliner chairs, and low tables. One had floor-to-ceiling bookshelves fully stocked with reading material. Another had a small kitchen carved into a corner.

Female laughter led her to a room at the end of the hall, but when she arrived, no one was there. More peals of laughter bubbled up. She leaned into the sound, searching for its source. At the end of the hall she encountered a circular staircase and wound her way upstairs.

"So this guy was, like, you know, saying that I had beautiful eyes, and I was like, what're you smokin', dude!"

More hilarious laughter.

Priscilla poked her head inside. The room fell quiet. "Hi, there," she said.

Four teenagers stared back at her. Not one returned the greeting.

"I'm Priscilla."

"Pri-scilla?" The young girl with vibrant brown eyes said her name like a scowl. "What kind of name is *that*?"

"My mother always thought it sounded like royalty."

Another girl, this one with stringy strawberry-blonde hair, crossed her arms. "Sounds snooty." Her eye roll much more pronounced than it needed to be.

A girl with dark chocolate skin stuck out her lip and shrugged. "I like it. Sounds all girly-girl."

Priscilla smiled. "May I come in?"

"Yeah, whatever," the brown-eyed girl said.

She stepped inside, ever aware of the flush of estrogen in the room. Her eyes struggled to take in the various kinds of makeup, the brushes and combs, the products—most of them low-end toxic sprays and lotions that would do more harm than good to the girls' locks.

"What are you—a teacher?" the strawberry-blonde asked.

"Actually, I'm a hairdresser."

"Yeah, I figured that. Your hair is kinda perfect." She said that with a turned-up nose.

"So you don't like my hair?"

The girl shrugged. "It's fine. You just look rich."

"I see." She paused. "What are your names?"

When no one answered right away, the brown-eyed girl spoke up, leading the introductions. "I'm Mari." She pointed around the room to the strawberry-blonde, the dark-skinned beauty, and the blonde-haired girl that had yet to say anything. "And that's Amber, Staci, and Morgan."

"You from around here?" Amber asked.

"No, I'm from Virginia. I just moved here a few months ago, well, to the beach."

"See? I told you Priscilla was rich."

Though an invisible wall had been erected in the room, Priscilla determined to lower it, inch by inch. "I'll tell you something I've never told my new friends in California," she said.

"What's that?" Mari wore suspicion on her face.

Priscilla laughed. "Well, when I was young, the kids in my neighborhood called me Cilla.'"

"That's much better than *Priscilla*," Amber said.

Priscilla laughed. "I figured you'd like that."

"So if you're a hairdresser, what are you doing here?" Staci asked. "Did you come to teach us about hair?"

"Yeah, Amber can do braids real good—" Morgan said.

"But only certain kinds." Staci quirked her head to the side, assessing Priscilla. "Want to teach us other kinds?"

"If you'd like, I can do that."

Nearly the entire time they talked, Morgan was holding her hair up with one hand. "I wish I could put my hair up."

"Well, you certainly could."

Morgan frowned. "I don't have the profile for it."

Priscilla laughed. "Oh, honey. I've heard that so many times, it isn't funny." She stood and walked over to the girl, then gently reached for the spray of hair she held above her head. "May I?"

Morgan released a dramatic sigh, her shoulders drooping. "Okay."

As Priscilla set out to make a messy bun out of Morgan's hair, she talked her way throughout. "Part your hair as normal, like so," she said. "Then use your fingers to make a line down behind your part. You'll want to leave these front pieces hanging in front, okay?"

The other girls began to step closer, peering over the process.

"Then use your finger and thumb to create a hole at the top of your ponytail, like this." She demonstrated and waited for all of them to acknowledge that they understood. "Now here's the fun part. You'll want to flip your ponytail upward like this and stick it right into the hole you made. Then pull it all the way through."

"Oh, that's cool," Staci said.

"Isn't it?" Priscilla grinned. "Okay, Staci, reach into my bag over there—I should have done that first—and pull out the pink zippered bag. Inside you'll find bobby pins and some small elastic circles."

Staci rummaged through the bag and found the elements Priscilla asked for. "I have a whole bunch of 'em in my hand."

"Good. Now, we're going to repeat the process a couple of times, like this." She continued to demonstrate, patiently anchoring several layers of ponytails and flipping them upward. When she was done, she said, "Now let's create a bun by rolling the last ponytail into a circle. But first, Morgan's hair is long, so I'm going to put some bands on the last ponytail, like so."

She stood back for a few seconds, holding up the secured ponytail so they could all see what she had done.

"Finally, we'll roll up the last ponytail over the others, and secure them with the bobby pins. I think about six should do it."

When she was finished, she stepped back. "Voila! What do you think?"

While the other girls examined her work, Morgan was

turning side to side, doing her best to see the back of her head in the mirror.

"Can I borrow your phone to take a pic?" Amber asked Priscilla.

"Great idea." She pulled it out of her pocket, unlocked it, and handed it over.

Amber took the photo then showed it to Morgan, who gushed, "I love it!"

Wade popped his head inside the room. "Hello, ladies."

"Hi."

"Hey."

"What's up, Wade."

He grinned at the various greetings, then caught Priscilla's eye. "Are you ready to go, Priscilla?"

"She's Cilla," Amber said.

Wade's eyes widened. "Well, okay then. Ready, Cilla?"

Reluctantly, she said her goodbyes and together they took the stairs down to the first floor.

"Sorry to have to leave you alone," Wade said. "Did you get enough of a look around?"

"For now, yes."

He hesitated. "Listen, I've got to get back to my office, but you are welcome to come out here anytime you like. It is somewhat of a drive, however."

"No problem, Wade." She began walking toward the exit. "I'll talk, you drive."

Minutes later they were on their way back to the coast.

Wade switched on smooth jazz, the instrumental music feeding their quiet thoughts until Priscilla spoke up. "I would like to volunteer at the center."

"Like I said, if you don't mind the drive, you can visit anytime."

She shook her head. "That's not what I meant. I want to really get involved." She swiveled around in her seat, her gestures animated. "I can teach the girls how to do their hair."

"Their hair."

"Yes. How to braid it—oh, you know there are so many kinds of braids."

"I did not know that."

She frowned. "Don't be a man right now."

He coughed a laugh. "What?"

"Seriously, Wade, there are all kinds of braids: snake, waterfall, Dutch, and of course, French. And all kinds of 'updos' too. I want to be there for them to, basically, answer their questions about hairstyles and hygiene."

"I'm sure they'd love that."

She nodded once. "It's settled then. On another subject, are you aware of the way Candace looks at you?"

He turned down the music. "Excuse me? What did you just say?"

"Candace. She's quite interested in you."

"That is ... so far from being true."

Priscilla leaned her head back and gaped at him. "You're oblivious. But that's better than giving someone the cold shoulder outright. I will say, though, that maybe a girlfriend would be good for you, Wade. Might soften some of those edges.

"Are you trying to fix me? Do I look like I need fixing?"

"I like people to be happy."

"Not everyone finds their satisfaction in happiness."

"Oh no? Then why are you driving like a maniac?"

He laughed. "What?"

"You're speeding now and I can tell it makes you exceedingly happy."

He glanced at his dashboard, and by the sound of the engine, he was easing up on the gas pedal. "There. Happy?"

"You mean do I feel as if I might live? Then, yes, I'm quite happy."

Wade wagged his head.

"So, as I was saying ... where do you find your happiness, Wade? I mean, other than in your maniacal driving habits."

He sputtered a little, obviously agitated, though she couldn't fathom why. "I find it in my work," he said, "in making progress on my pursuits. Those kinds of things."

"That's not happiness—that's simply coping."

"Really. So in addition to your cosmetology license, you have a degree in psychology now?"

She brushed the air with a hand. "That was rude."

He swallowed, his Adam's apple bouncing. "Sorry."

"Listen, I know what it's like to bury yourself in work, travel—you name it. But what helps me more is quite simply looking for the bright side. Looking forward helps me overcome rather than dwelling on the sins of yesterday."

He gave her a sideways glance. "You don't look like someone who's faced much adversity."

"My husband left me."

The words dropped from her mouth starkly against the dark night. She wasn't looking for sympathy, but she sensed something was bothering Wade, and it very well didn't help for him to think that her life was as rosy as it may have looked.

"I'm sorry to hear that," he said. "Is there any chance for a reconciliation?"

"He left me for my neighbor, well, *our* neighbor. Then they had a baby together." She glanced out the window, the terrain in shadows. "Taking him back isn't an option."

"I understand." He paused. "I hadn't realized you were married before."

"The ironic thing is I always wanted children, but he did not."

"So you agreed."

"Agreed to what? Not have children?"

He glanced at her. "I apologize. It was not my place to ask."

"It was a fair question, since I was the one who brought this up."

He nodded.

She sighed. "That's complicated. But ultimately, marriage isn't about always getting what one wants."

He glanced over at her. "I've never been married, so excuse me if I am overstepping here, but it must have been difficult to hide the desire for something as life changing as children."

She shrugged, suddenly tired. Maybe divulging personal information from her past hadn't been such a grand idea after all. "You know what they say ... *c'est la vie*. I've found a new life here, so I have nothing to complain about."

"Are you happy?"

"Darling, I live near the sea with friends who have become like family to me. What's not to love?" She put a smile on her face, which made her feel better already. "Okay, now that I've told you something personal, how about you?"

"How about me what?"

"Tell me something about you, Wade Prince."

"You mean other than what you know already—that I had my heart broken publicly?"

"Just a blip on an otherwise fascinating life, I'm sure. What else have you got?"

He chuckled. "That's one way to look at it." He inhaled

roughly before speaking again. "Fine. Here's something: the charity is out of money."

"Oh no. Now, that's tragic news. But it's not exactly personal, now is it."

"It is when you believe in something wholeheartedly and it is struggling to keep its doors open."

"I can see that. Yes, absolutely. What happened?"

His expression turned grim. "A major sponsor reneged."

"That's terrible. But surely there is something that can be done? Is there a plan to recoup what has been lost? Perhaps some fundraisers? An auction—I'm sure the inn would donate a weekend stay or two. Or perhaps, sell bricks with people's names on them?"

He peered at her, a smile forming. "You really do look on the bright side of things, don't you?"

"Well, darling, you need a plan if you're going to turn this around. Do you have one? Sophia runs social media campaigns all the time for her fashion line. Perhaps you could talk to her."

Wade released a sigh. "That's not necessary. The plan I have for the center is more ... personal."

"Oh good. So you have a plan."

"Yes. Yes, I do."

A pop of relief settled within her, but it was temporary. Now that she'd seen the center and had been inspired by its potential for growth, she hated to see it fade away. She stole another glance at Wade. His eyes were on the road, the firm set of his jaw illuminated by passing traffic. Gently, she asked, "What are you going to do?"

"For starters," he said, "I'm going to donate a million dollars."

~

WADE HOPED he wouldn't regret telling Priscilla his secret.

"A million dollars," she had repeated. "Well. If that's only for starters, I cannot wait to hear what else you've got up your sleeves."

The lack of surprise on her face told him that she did not believe him. Did she think he had been toying with her? He pondered that. It might be better to leave it that way. Maybe this was his "out."

She continued, a sober quality displayed in her profile. "Have you thought of how you will eat?"

"What do you mean?"

She turned to face him, bare concern on her face. "I mean, when you empty out your savings. I can't imagine you'd have much left to live on after pouring a million bucks into the center—as noble as that is. Unless I'm being presumptuous."

He stayed silent.

She squinted at him. "You mean you have more than a million in the bank?" When he didn't answer right away—did she really expect him to answer that?—she said, "How much more?"

"That's mighty forward of you, Ms. Cornwall."

"I'm inquisitive. Comes with being a hairdresser."

"There is the potential for more, yes."

"Wow."

"Yes."

This time, she fell silent. She watched him beneath eyelashes.

He cut into the quiet. "Best not to spread that around."

His cellphone rang and he glanced at it on its stand,

sensing a scowl creeping onto his face. Laura was calling but he let it go to voicemail.

"So," Priscilla continued, "how did you acquire a million extra dollars ... may I ask?"

"The old-fashioned way."

She continued to stare at him.

"You know, hard work. Good investments. ADHD."

She laughed now. "What does that mean?"

"It means I don't stop much."

"As in, you don't sleep?"

"True. And I don't usually discuss my financial state with ..."

"Strangers?"

He paused. "Do not be offended. Let me explain." He exhaled. "I own a building in New York with other investors. Right now we are working on selling it to a developer with incredible plans for the neighborhood, but the deal is contingent on them convincing the entire block to sell. They are almost there."

"So does this mean you will be donating your proceeds to EduCenter?"

He turned slightly, one eye raised. "Part of them."

"So you'll be donating *part* of your proceeds?"

"Right."

"And it's a sure thing?"

A knife of tension had been in his back since the onset of this deal. Her question turned it slightly. "Nothing is a sure thing, but I believe the developer will succeed."

"What happens if he doesn't?"

"You ask *a lot* of questions."

"I find all of this fascinating, but if you would rather not divulge ..."

He exhaled. "The building needs work. Over time it has come to our attention that, should we hold onto the property much longer, we will have many repairs to complete—expensive ones."

"So this deal will be quite a blessing for you."

He relaxed his grip on the steering wheel. "Yes."

"Then, for your sake—and the center's sake—I hope it all goes well for you." She smiled at him. "I'll pray for you."

"Thank you."

"And I will also pray you get some sleep." She laughed when she said this.

He leaned toward her, his voice a whisper. "So now you know something personal about me."

"What? That you don't sleep much?"

He might have allowed her to think that's exactly what he meant, but she continued, "Or that you're a millionaire?"

He pressed his lips into a line for a moment. "Something like that."

Slowly, she turned. "Wait ... just how rich will this deal make you, Wade?" Laughter bubbled out of her, the sound of it infectious. "Don't tell me it'll make you one of those *billionaires*."

He narrowed his eyes. "What do you mean 'one of those'?"

Priscilla leaned against the door of the car and stared at him with an incredulous smile riding on her face. "Like a hero in a romance novel." She paused. "Wade Prince, are you on your way to becoming a billionaire?"

"Let's just say ... I'm working on it."

∽

PRISCILLA HADN'T ALWAYS PLANNED on being a hairdresser. Not

at all. Her parents, long retired in Miami—a cliché, but true—each had ideas of what she should become. Her mother thought, perhaps, a ballerina, while her father believed she had the focus and boldness to become a lawyer.

Dance classes lasted until about third grade. And she got over the thrill of arguing in public when Norma Eaton poked her sharpened claws at her after their teacher, Mr. Franz, declared her the debate winner in ninth grade English. They'd debated the merits of baked macaroni and cheese versus PB&Js in the school cafeteria. She, of course, won on the side of mac 'n' cheese.

Priscilla's shears moved deftly across Jackson's full-bodied hair, her cutting tool an extension of her hands. She snipped and shaped, scissor over comb, trepidation long ago replaced by confidence. After training as a stylist, she put in hundreds of additional hours learning barbering skills—and she never looked back. She loved her work, the creativity in it, the resulting satisfaction on the faces of her clients.

"Shew," said Katrina, who swept the clippings from around her chair across the room. "I'll say it again—those are some mad barbering skills you've got, girl."

Priscilla smiled at her co-worker. "Thanks, beautiful."

In the mirror, she noticed Jackson's eyes snap away from his phone, a confused look on his face. Priscilla winked at him. "You're beautiful, too."

Katrina cackled.

Jackson gave her a lopsided grin. "Guess you weren't talking about me, were you?"

"I'll tell you who's beautiful," Katrina said. "That Wade Prince is yum-my." She shook her head. "That stud was in here earlier and—woo!—what eye candy he is."

Jackson gave Katrina a quizzical stare through the mirror. "Aren't you a happily married woman, K?"

"Yes, sir. What's your point?"

Priscilla held back a laugh. She switched to clippers and began evening out Jackson's sideburns.

"Anyhoo," Katrina continued, "that Wade was sitting over there in Manuel's chair earlier looking like he just walked off a movie set, all primped and camera-ready—even before he got a haircut."

Jackson shook his head and Priscilla yelped. "Whoa there. I've got sharp scissors in my hand, boss."

He grinned. "Sorry about that."

They fell into the lull of listening to instrumental spa music as Jackson returned to engaging with his phone and she continued to shape his wavy hair.

When she had been with Wade the day before, he hadn't mentioned anything about coming into the spa today. Was he avoiding her? She still didn't know what to make of the truth bomb he had dropped into their conversation on the way home. The one about writing a million-dollar check to the center once the building deal went through. *If* it went through.

Priscilla paused. It wasn't every day that she was tooling around the state with a man on his way to becoming a billionaire. Actually, that was more of a never-day occurrence. Not that it changed how she felt about him—he was still a good-looking, but somewhat irascible, guy who confounded her every time she encountered him.

Her hands slowed. "That's quite the scar you have hidden away up here," she said to Jackson. "Does it have a good story to go with it?"

"Ah, yes. I was skateboarding down a perilously steep hill

when I took a corner too fast and ended up rolling down the face of a sheer cliff."

She put her poker face on.

He glanced at her in the mirror. "Not buying it, are you?"

"Nope."

He chuckled. "I tripped over my untied shoes when I was a teen. Mom had warned me, but I had to learn the hard way."

She nodded, smiling. "Don't we all."

Laughter bubbled up from them both until Priscilla's mind trailed to a scar of her own, from a procedure she had undergone long ago, something she almost never thought about. She swallowed, burying that thought. "So," she said, keeping her tone light, "what do you know about Wade's love life?"

Jackson curled his upper lip. "Guys don't talk about stuff like that."

"Ha. Sure. Okay."

"You question me? Your boss?"

"Oh, my. You're playing the boss card. In that case, I give up."

"You give up to easy. Okay, fine. I'll tell you what I know."

She shrugged, her smile lighthearted. "If you must."

"You already know about his former relationship with Sophia, of course. What else do you want to know?"

"Oh, I don't know ... well, has he ever dated anyone else, to your recollection?"

"Hm. I vaguely remember someone a long time ago. I think she worked for him. I was probably in high school then. She had short black hair and her name was like a flower."

"Oh, really. Was it Petunia? Daisy? Lily?"

He shrugged and raised two open palms. "That's all I got. How about you?"

"Me, what?"

"Are you interested in Wade? That is why you are asking about him. Right?"

She opened her mouth to answer him, but Meg strolled in before the words would form.

Meg bent down and gave her husband a smack of her lips onto his cheek. She hovered there, smiling at him in the mirror though they were only inches apart. "Did you just try to set up Priscilla with Wade?"

Jackson sputtered, as if aghast—an act, obviously.

Meg's animated brown eyes opened wide, and she turned her head, gazing up over her shoulder at Priscilla. "It's an amazing idea, actually."

Priscilla shook her head. "Uh, thank you, but *no*. Wade is a good man, I'll give you that. But, to be very honest, he reminds me too much of my curmudgeonly ex-husband. Goodness! I've had enough of that attitude to contend with for a lifetime." Meg stepped back as Priscilla unlatched the neck of Jackson's cape and removed it from him, careful not to dump freshly snipped hairs onto his suit. She shrugged as she folded the cape. "I was just curious about him. That's all."

Meg gave her a sweet side hug. "Aw, because you just don't like to see anyone unhappy."

Priscilla nodded and caught eyes with her friend. "Beneath that crust is a lost soul, I'm thinking."

After Meg and Jackson had gone, Priscilla set about the mundane task of sweeping around her chair. She liked this part more than others in her position did. In fact, many salons left this for their assistant to handle, which she often did as well.

But she also found that as her arms worked to tidy her space, her mind had opportunity to expand. She came up with some of her best ideas during mindless, circular sweeping. A smile curled on Priscilla's face. Wasn't she sweeping up a mop of curly hair when the idea to move west popped into her mind?

The recollection churned within her. She'd had a full life in Virginia. A job. Clients. A routine. But something ... something was missing. She'd heard about a writer at the inn—Meg's inn—who wrote an entire novel from inside one of those gorgeous suites overlooking the ocean, and she had to come. To find her own happiness.

She slowed the broom, her fingers holding it tighter. Was she happy? She asked this of herself, just as Wade had the day before. She had deftly sidestepped his question then, wondering, was this all she wanted? To be happy? And really, what did that entail?

The broom stopped. She had come here to find her life again, but maybe wholeness was more than pasting on a happy face while running away from the deep ache of severe wounds.

Maybe ... it was something deeper.

Priscilla inhaled and blew out a slow, deliberate breath, glad that, for the moment, she was alone in the salon. Her mind drifted to Wade, her acquaintance and almost-friend. Though she questioned whether he had found contentment in his life, she knew he'd found purpose.

Slowly, she nodded, a dawning coming from a deep place.

Who knew what the future held? Whether her longing for love, for children, for something more would ever come to be? One thing she knew was that she would *not* be falling in love with Wade Prince. She could admire him from afar and that was fine with her.

But ... could it be that she might find her purpose in the charity he had helped to found? She began moving that broom again, ideas formulating that made her very, very happy.

∼

WADE SAT at his desk in the west wing of the second floor of his home, recalling the conversation he'd had with Priscilla the day before. For a long time he had kept his business and personal life private, tucked away from inquiring eyes. But last night, that all changed.

The large casement windows had been flung open, and even from up here on the hillside, the briskness of sea air could be felt. The report on his desk should have been done by now, but he had been lost in thought, ever since arriving home from EduCenter. A recurring picture of Rose, his former administrative assistant, kept drifting through his head. She was delivering a file to him—along with a coy smile.

He shut down the memory.

This was not like him. His mind did not wander. Especially when it should be keenly focused on getting the New York property sold and the money re-invested.

Wade scratched his head, noting the shorn feel of his hair. Sheepishness washed over him. He had dashed into the inn's salon this morning, before Priscilla's shift, and had Manuel cut his hair.

Now that some time had passed, he wondered if she would hear that he had stopped in. And if she did find out, would she think he was avoiding her? Would that matter?

He quirked his cheek, feeling quite surly.

Priscilla had been forthright and confident yesterday, kind to the girls she met, and downright inquisitive all the way home. Her questioning needled him, and yet, he wasn't particularly bothered that she had spoken her mind.

He thought back on their conversation in the car. She had not answered his question to her, the one about being happy. Instead, she stated all the good. He admired her for looking on the positive, something he knew he should try to do more himself. But she was still somewhat of a mystery to him. Her story was a sad one, and he recognized her tenacity to pick up and move across the country for a new life. He thought on that. Perhaps he should have asked her if her move was all she had hoped it would be.

Some of her questions to him had dug into a place he didn't quite feel like considering.

And suddenly he knew the reason his mind had drifted to Rose. When Priscilla began to press the notion that Candace showed some kind of interest in him, he had shut her down. First of all, he didn't see it. The woman had been nothing but professional in his presence. But if truth be told, he had been involved in an "office romance" before, and the memory of that time was not particularly ... stellar.

He raked a hand through his newly shorn hair and blew out a sigh. Years ago, and against his better judgment, Wade had dated Rose, an admin in his office. She had loose curls of black hair and a smattering of freckles across her nose. A pixie who had captured him with homemade cookies and her love of driving along the coast.

She had never once complained about his driving speed.

That may have been the one thing she didn't complain about. He recalled the time he had invited her to his home for a home-cooked dinner. He took a Saturday off, an unheard-of reality for him, and made a slow-roasted prime rib dinner.

When she walked into his home, modest by some of his

contemporaries' standards, she quickly scanned his kitchen. "Where is your cook?"

He had pulled her toward him, wrapping his arms around her. "You're looking at him."

Rose inclined her head, her mouth pouting. "You cook for yourself? I'm surprised."

He'd laughed at the time, taking her comments as teasing. But after a while, he began to notice how she turned up her nose at venues that were anything less than high-end.

Like the time he pulled into the parking lot of an iconic shrimp and fish place near Malibu. A line snaked out the door as diners waited to place their orders. He killed the engine and unlatched his seatbelt, but when he turned to look at Rose, she was frowning.

"Doesn't seem very appetizing," she said.

He kissed her cheek. "Give it a try. I know you're going to love the food here."

They'd sat on a wooden bench eating fish 'n' chips while taking in the blues and pinks of the coastal sky. Rose had hardly said a word all during their meal, and he had assumed she was tired. Until he overheard her complain to his bookkeeper, Tonia, about the low-brow place he had taken her. So embarrassing, she had said.

That was around the time he realized that cupid's arrow had apparently pierced his heart *and* his head. It turned out that Rose was Tonia's niece. And Tonia had, apparently, shared confidential information with Rose about his financial status.

Seemed that Rose's interest in him went only as far as he could bankroll.

He had gazed into Rose's eyes, expecting to see layers of

love staring back at him, but all he found was betrayal. And it had ripped a hole in him.

After that, he fired both Rose and Tonia. Then he buried his head deeper into his work. Invested in a redevelopment property in Brooklyn. Helped form a first-time home buyer funding venture. Helped Riley Holdings, the company Jackson —and Sophia—inherited, get its firm footing back.

And right about that time, he fell hard again. As a fashion designer, Sophia was a business owner in her own right. She had faced adversity with grace and a whole lot of dignity. To be fair, he'd known about her—and what she had been through—from her brother. Plus, he had known her father, William, a good man.

Suddenly, he couldn't remember what he had against relationships in the first place. So, he pursued her. He pursued *them*—as a couple.

Wade rocked back against his chair, his arms folded in front of him. How long had he even given Sophia to settle in to her new life here in California before he chased after her like a besotted puppy?

He shook his head. Wade did not have time for this. Too many unfinished projects. Emails to answer. Calls to return. If he just put his head down and did his work, got on top of it all, he would find satisfaction ... his purpose. That was all he needed.

CHAPTER 5

Tepid sweat seeped across her brow and upper lip. To her fingers' touch, her cheeks swam, clammy. Priscilla rocked her head side to side, a cry grappling within her throat as it attempted to become free. The dark, guttural moan scraped along the interior of her neck and emerged into the bright morning, waking her as it did.

She sat up. Priscilla held a hand to her cheek, caught between a memory that kept her anchored to her past and the new day that dawned before her.

She glanced out the window, remembering the minor surgery she'd had. If it had worked, who knew what her life would look like now?

"Are you almost ready?"

She nodded her yes.

"As a reminder, we'll go in and make a small incision," the doctor said. *"With your good health and level of fitness, you should be up and back at life within a couple of weeks. Probably sooner."*

. . .

She remembered the hope that had ballooned within her at the thought of fixing her infertility issues. Not that anything had ever been proven in that regard. But when Leo had finally agreed to try for a child and nothing happened, the doctor had a hunch. She was hopeful that the procedure he was proposing would take care of it.

Priscilla closed her eyes, breathed deeply, and tried to shake off the memory. She slid out of bed, slipped her feet into a pair of furry slippers that she'd found on one of her excursions to Florida to visit her parents. The softness of those slippers invited her back into the present, the feel of them comforting against her skin.

She tucked a pod into her espresso machine, virtually patting herself on the back for splurging on this gift after she moved. Admitting her addiction to caffeine was the first step, she reasoned. So, instead of spending dollars daily at a high-end coffee house, she could make it herself.

With the espresso brewing, she padded over to the small window seat that overlooked a greenbelt and park. This rental condo was small and pricey—just about everything was by the coast. But what sold it for her was the seat that looked out onto a small park. There she saw everyday life: dogs and their owners, couples and solitary walkers, children climbing all over playground equipment.

The picture of idyllic living.

She retrieved her espresso, gave it a shot of cream, and returned to the window. If she were ever told she had to give up coffee in the mornings, her fallback would be to inhale it instead. Maybe the aroma alone would be enough to wake her up in the mornings. She laughed at the thought and admonished herself to drink up, and as she did, another less hopeful memory made its way back into her mind.

"YOU HAVE A RARE BLOOD TYPE. Do you have any family members with O negative who we could ask to give blood?" her doctor asked.

"I don't understand. Why would they need to do that?"

"It's just a precaution. If for some reason you needed a blood transfusion during the surgery, then we'd have it at the ready. I'd ask you to give us some of your own blood, but I'd prefer not to with the medication I have you on."

"I see. Well, my husband has the same blood type as I do."

"Perfect," he said. "Ask him to come in as soon as possible. We'll take some blood and test it, and if you don't need it—I don't think you will—then we will give it to the blood bank."

PRISCILLA TOOK a long sip of her hot coffee, drawing deeply of the memory of that time. She had gone home and asked Leo to go back to the hospital with her to give blood.

But he balked.

"NOT MY THING," he said. He kissed her temple. "Hey, I'll be there when you wake up and I'll drive you home and fix us some dinner. Anything you want, babe, but"—he screwed up his face and stuck out his tongue like he'd just tasted cod liver oil—"you know I can't stand needles."

PRISCILLA TOOK another look out the window at the lush park that teemed with life. Turned out, she had the procedure but never had a chance to find out if it had solved the issue—soon after, she learned of Leo's infidelity.

She had come a long way, and not just in miles. As Priscilla took another sip, she determined to lock unfavorable memories away ... for good.

∽

A WEEK OF DEADLINES, phone calls, and all-around burying his head in work had passed. As he drove out to the center for his weekly Money Smart class, Wade's cell phone rang.

"Hello, Candace." He purposely forced thoughts of Priscilla's hunch about the woman out of his mind.

"I wanted to give you a heads-up about something."

"Shoot."

"Your friend, you know, Priscilla? Well, she's here. I hope that's okay."

His pulse revved slightly before plummeting. "Did she say why?"

"Oh, yes, of course. She asked if she could come out to teach some of the girls to braid their hair—remember how some of them asked last time? I said yes, of course, and I want you to know she's been fingerprinted."

"I see."

"Of course, there hasn't been time for processing, and then I realized you were coming out today too, and, well, I second-guessed myself." She paused. "Should I have called you or one of the other board members first?"

Wade pictured her in the lounge with the teens, her red hair flowing behind her, laughter on her face. The girls would likely be crowded around her. He pictured Amber, Morgan, Staci, and Mari as they clambered for Priscilla's attentions.

Inexplicably, his thoughts faded to a dark shade. What did she want from him?

Candace's voice cut in. "The board is always saying that the thing we're lacking other than money is—"

"Volunteers," they said in unison.

"No need to call me," Wade said, finally. "If I introduce you to someone who I am also introducing to the kids, you can consider that my endorsement."

Candace sighed, relief in her voice. "Thank you. That's what I was thinking, truly. She seems to be doing fine without a lot of input from me, which is perfect since I have to meet with the drywall contractor this afternoon."

"That's right. The plumbing issue."

"The leak in the kitchen has been taken care of, thankfully. But the damage to the wall is going to take some work."

And money, Wade thought. He pulled the car into the lot behind the building that housed the girls' lounge. Right now they would probably be talking about hair and other girlish essentials, and though he wouldn't admit it readily, he had parked here on purpose.

"Thank you for your call, Candace. I will stop by your office after my meeting with the board."

He hung up, but lingered. Rather than exit his car, Wade sat for a moment, watching Priscilla's shadowy yet unmistakable figure through a window. One of the girls—Amber, perhaps?—sat still as "Cilla" worked with her hair like it was moldable art. Her hands moved with fluidity, one of them occasionally accenting the air with animated gestures. The other girls encircled her, yet gave her space. He smiled. Priscilla exuded confidence and poise, her lively demonstration drawing the girls out of their usual screen-induced trance.

Maybe her sudden interest in the center had less to do with him, and more to do about ... her. He couldn't move, his mind turning his thoughts over as he watched Priscilla speak to the girls.

Suddenly and with a flourish he did not see coming, she grabbed Amber's braid—or was it a ponytail?—and yanked. Hard. He squinted, jutting his face closer to his windshield. Was she ... was she really grabbing the young girl's hair with all her strength? Yanking her upward, as if to make an example of her? Wade's fist clenched. He exited his car and threw shut the door, questioning himself as he did. Hadn't he just concluded that Priscilla's presence at the center was perfectly natural? Welcome, even?

Had he lost his mind allowing a stranger such access to the girls?

He pushed open the front doors and stalked down the hallway toward the girls' lounge. He should have told Candace that the drywall could wait, that she needed to keep an eye on things. Wade barreled through the lounge door, his lungs clenching, not bothering to knock, which was his usual protocol when entering the girls' space.

The door, flung open now, hit the wall behind it with a *thwack*. Screams filled his ear, the girls crowded around Priscilla, and they were ... laughing?

Priscilla stood in the midst of them, a hand on her hip while her other hand held up a torso-less head by a long, thick braid, high in the air. She turned at the sound of him entering the room, a triumphant smile on her face.

That smile of hers assessed him somehow. Relief and a bout of nausea rolled through his gut. "What ... what's going on here?" he said.

She tucked that body-less head into the crook of one arm

and cocked her hip like she held a basketball. "I didn't know you'd be here today, Wade." She swept a gaze over the girls and back to him. "The girls and I were working on our styling skills."

"Oh-ha-ha!" Amber said, breaking from the pack. "You thought she was tearing one of our heads off!"

Staci and Morgan collapsed onto bean bags chairs, tears accompanying their screams and chortles. Amber pointed at Wade, his expression open and gaping, and Mari followed after her, the two of them hopping and shouting over one another.

"I know it's true," Amber said, barely able to get the words out. "I saw you sitting in your car, staring at us."

Priscilla tilted her head to one side, that smile on her face teasing. "Is this true, Mr. Prince? Did you think that I, uh ..."?

"Decapitated one of us! Hahahaha ..." Amber put her head on Priscilla's shoulder, tears streaming down her freckled cheeks. "That's the best, Cilla."

He felt ... exposed. Annoyed. Embarrassed. But as he watched the pandemonium of cheerfulness in what was often a rather somber room punctuated with fits of sarcasm, he could not help but roll his own eyes at his knee-jerk take on Priscilla's teaching skills.

Wade shook his head, unable to conceal his smile, albeit a self-deprecating one. "All right, settle down," he said, unable to look as stern as he attempted to sound.

Priscilla turned her full attention to the girls and handed the mannequin head to Staci, who promptly placed it back on a stand that looked much like a tripod. The girl sighed. "Best day ever."

As he backed out of the room, Wade's smile faded. Why had he jumped to conclusions like that? The girls had seen right through him. And Priscilla? Undoubtedly, she questioned his ability to reason. He rubbed a hand across the back of his neck, soothing away the ache that had settled there.

Wade began to sense fissures in the protection he had built around himself, and he did not like that one bit. From the moment he had met Priscilla out on the inn's lawn, warning flags had alerted him to be on his guard. She seemed ... well, too good to be true. Now as he thought back on the ridiculous way he burst into the girls' lounge, he wondered if perhaps he had been hoping to prove himself right.

∼

WELL, that was something ... else. Priscilla pressed her lips together, a curl of laughter rising. Wade had barreled into the room with mental guns drawn.

So dramatic.

Maybe she should have mentioned to him that she had planned to come out here to meet with the girls. But she hadn't seen him lately, so was alerting the press expected? She glanced around the room as the girls packed up their things. Once the idea of getting involved here, of putting feet to her thoughts, had entered her head, there was no turning back.

Pretty much the way she'd lived her life for as long as she could remember.

Amber caught her eye.

"Have you changed your mind?" Priscilla asked her.

"Yeah. I think so." The strawberry blonde tilted her head to the side, eyeing herself in the mirror. "I mean, you could try. If you want to."

"Absolutely." Priscilla patted a chair. "Here. Sit."

Amber plopped into the chair. The other girls took notice and put their things down again.

"You gonna get a waterfall braid?" Staci asked.

Amber glanced at Priscilla, her eyes upturned and questioning.

"That's exactly what I'm going to do," Priscilla said. "Watch closely. I'll talk through the steps so that you can all learn how to do this."

She parted Amber's hair and gathered a thick section. "Okay, so here I'm going to divide this section into three parts."

The girls all leaned forward, observing.

"We'll start with the back piece, cross it over the middle like this." She demonstrated. "Then take the front section and cross it over the middle next."

She moved slowly through the process, careful to allow each of the girls enough time to learn what she was doing. They watched as she continued as she had started, and added hair to each new strand, creating a French braid.

"Okay, now here's where you need to pay extra attention." She held up the section of Amber's hair that she was working on. "You'll want to drop this front section down now and pick up a strand of hair behind it instead. Okay? Now, cross it over the middle instead of that piece you just dropped down."

Several "oohs" punctuated the silence of the room. When she was finished, she brushed Amber's unbraided hair and turned her around. "Voila!"

"That's awesome!" Mari said.

Morgan clucked her tongue. "Piece of cake."

Priscilla leaned forward so her cheek was nearly touching Amber's. "What do you think? Do you like the look on you?"

Amber nodded. Her eyes glistened.

Priscilla frowned. "Is something wrong?" she whispered. "Do you want me to take it out?"

The door opened with a click and Wade stood at the entrance, quiet, his dark brows framing piercing eyes. Priscilla's throat caught and she looked away, back to the young girl who had shown unexpected emotion.

Quickly, Amber wiped her eyes with her fingers and shook her head. She jumped out of the chair and wrapped her arms around her waist.

"Are you ready to go?" Wade asked, oblivious to the moment he'd had a hand in ending. "I thought we could walk out together."

Priscilla swung a peek at Amber, who no longer looked as if she had just lost her favorite bracelet. Mari and Staci had slung their backpacks over their shoulders and were now examining Amber's hairstyle closely.

Wade cut in. "If you're ready, that is."

She grabbed her bag, said goodbye to the girls, and they walked out together. "You drove all the way out here for a pretty short meeting," she said to Wade as they strolled outside into the afternoon sun. In the short time that she had lived on California's central coast, she'd learned that the weather was far less predictable than points south. Or inland, for that matter. The summer heat outside of the center was stifling, but she could arrive home in under an hour and find a marine layer had moved in and she would have to pull on a sweater.

"I'm not actually leaving right now."

"No?"

He slowed his pace as they walked beneath the canopy of an evergreen. He leaned his head to one side, looking at her. She'd seen him do that before, but usually his eyes narrowed, as if scrutinizing something or someone. Priscilla had always figured this was one of the reasons for his success—he took his time considering all the angles about a deal before moving in.

He stopped and reached a hand to her elbow. This time, his gaze looked soft, his eyes round and inquiring. "I'm sorry that I—that I charged into the room like a madman."

She felt a little sorry for him now. "For the record, I would never characterize you as a madman."

"But?"

She smiled. "No buts. I wanted to clear that up. That's all."

He shifted. "But ... you do consider me to be difficult. I can see that in your eyes."

"You make me sound like I have been judging you." She shook her head. "If you knew me at all, Wade, you would know that I find it exhausting to live as judge and jury. That's not me."

He lifted his eyes from a downcast gaze. "Surely you have your opinions, though."

She laughed lightly now. "Of course I do, darling. We all do. The trick is knowing which ones matter enough to act on and which should be filed in a virtual shredder."

"That's quite a trick."

"It is."

"I can't say that I don't agree with what you've said, although I do find it difficult at times to upset the inertia of constant motion."

"Ah. There is where we are different. I crave rest as much as I crave purpose. They are not mutually exclusive, I have found."

His dark eyes startled. Wade watched her face, as if formulating a response in the pause. He leaned his forearm on the trunk of the tree, his expression wistful. "You may find this difficult to believe, but despite a schedule that does not include much in the form of rest, I agree with you."

"I can tell."

His eyes narrowed, but not in a condescending way. "Really? How so?"

"Look at the center, for example. The rest of the world sees a well-suited man marching by with a phone stuck in his ear, always working a deal. But these kids?"—she waved an open palm toward the building where directionless kids could find their way—"They light up around you and the people you have inspired to be here. They see someone who values purpose as much as laughter or rest, as you've given them that."

He shook his head. "I'm not a perfect guy."

"Well, darlin', I know that too."

He swung a full-mouthed smile at her. "See? You do have opinions in there. I knew it." He paused, still smiling, and darted a look around the tree-lined street before returning his attention to her. "There's a coffee place at the corner and I could use a cup. Join me before you leave?"

She agreed and they began to walk toward a strip mall several houses down from the center. The heat had zapped her appetite, but she liked the thought of a caffeine-infused iced coffee to keep her company on the ride home.

As they waited for their orders, Priscilla took a seat at a table toward the back that overlooked a wooden barrel overflowing with sweet peas. Corporate coffee had its perks, so to speak, but this place reminded her of climbing the steps up to her Aunt Jo's porch and slipping into the kitchen through the back door. The cafe even smelled liked home.

Wade handed Priscilla her coffee and took the seat across from her.

She didn't wait for an awkward moment to form. "You mentioned the other day that there were some funding issues with the center. Has the situation calmed some, I mean, after you've emptied your savings and all?"

He jerked a look at her. A smile settled on his face, as if he understood she was teasing.

"Seriously," she said. "Are things better?"

Wade took a long sip of his coffee. He set his cup down. "Somewhat. But let's not talk about that right now—tell me instead about your interest in EduCenter."

"It's not all that complicated, really. I have something to offer and the time to offer it, so I jumped in."

"There has to be more to it than that."

She gaped at him. "Why does there have to be?"

He took another swig of coffee. A delay tactic, perhaps?

She continued, "Now that we're done talking about me "

He coughed out a laugh. "Oh, is that what we're doing?"

"Why, yes, of course." She smiled openly at him now. "You mentioned you have a sister. Is she involved in the center?"

At the mention of his sister, Wade frowned. His gaze dropped to his cup, where it lingered in his hand. He blew out a sigh and returned his focus to her, though his expression had dulled some.

"Did I bring up something that you'd rather not talk about?"

He shook his head distractedly. "To answer your question, yes, my sister, Gwynnie, has at times visited the center. In fact, my niece, Sadie, is treated like a princess whenever she comes along."

"Rightly so."

"Yes," he said, his face deadpan, before recovering. "Actually, I'm in the doghouse with her right now."

"I can't imagine why." She was good at deadpanning too.

He pointed at her briefly. "You know, if you were one of my employees I would have to consider firing you for such a remark."

"Well, then, good thing I'm happily employed."

"Here's the thing: My sister had a disastrous marriage. I never wanted her to marry her husband, though I'm glad she did because my niece is an incredible creature."

"But you still don't like that she ignored your advice about marrying him in the first place."

His eyes caught with hers. She knew she had drawn a trickle of blood.

"The bottom line is that Dak—her ex—squandered the money our father left us."

"While you turned yours into millions."

"Now you're making me sound like a jackass."

She gave him a kind smile. "I'm just trying to understand."

"I wish she would have stood up to him. Better yet, why didn't she come to me? I could have advised her—she knows I would have."

"Did he bully her in any way?"

Those dark eyes of his turned even darker. "Not in the way you mean."

"How do I mean?"

"He didn't beat her. I would have known and I would have taken care of it."

"Sounds like that would have involved cannoli or something," she said in her best imitation.

Wade turned an incredulous look on her. Understanding

appeared to dawn and with it, a small smile. "Like that scene in *The Godfather*. Right."

"I'm not talking only about a physical act, Wade. Some foes can be quite subtle in their mistreatment."

His smile faded and he stared at her for a long beat. She surmised that she'd said too much, the conversation becoming too personal, uncomfortable.

When he didn't respond, she added, "I wish your sister the best as she moves on. Who knows? Maybe we'll have a chance to meet sometime."

"Gwynnie would like you. I can see that you are on her side already."

Priscilla rolled her eyes, unconcerned with how "unladylike" it may have looked. "Please. I'm not taking sides here. All I can say is that we all have different strengths. Your sister was a working mother—pretty heroic if you ask me. Maybe she thought her husband was honorable and that he would do for her what she didn't have time or energy to do for herself."

Wade didn't reply, but Priscilla couldn't seem to stop herself. It was as if she were on some type of roll. "Really, Wade. How is it different from you handing over a million bucks to EduCenter in its time of need?"

"It's not the same."

She pursed her lips and stared him down for a beat. "Here's how I see it," she said, finally.

He scoffed, his eyes lively. "Oh so now you're going to tell me how you see it?"

She leaned forward, pointing at him. "Seriously. Your sister trusted her husband. If I'm not mistaken, you said they married in church. Was it a Christian ceremony?"

"How would that matter?"

"Well, darling, that means he promised to love her as

Christ loves the Church. And that means Christ would not steal from her. She trusted him, and he failed her. It's on him."

She sat back triumphant.

He considered her, his eyes unwavering, the telltale sign he gave when he was mulling something intensely. Finally, he began, "I wish ..."

"You wish?"

The unwavering eyes gave way to a flash of defeat. "That things had been different."

"Don't we all?" She exhaled and slowly shook her head. "We can't redo anything but we can grab opportunities to start fresh."

He drained his coffee cup, his eyes trained on hers. "Like moving across the country to the best coast."

She stared back at him. "Something like that."

CHAPTER 6

Priscilla released her wavy red hair from a silk scrunchie, allowing it to cascade onto her shoulders. The waves rolled in fiercely tonight, but she welcomed their energy. The sun began its descent, but still had a way to go before bidding adieu. She walked along the meandering path, allowing the surge of salt-coated air to revive her.

Truthfully, her feet were killing her, but so were her hands. The new intern, Edna, accidentally spilled an entire jar of Barbicide on the counter where Priscilla had been sprucing up her cuticles between clients. Priscilla shut her eyes tightly. How was the poor girl to know that the stuff could burn skin? That it was meant to clean combs and should always—as in *always*—be diluted with water first?

She made a mental note to ask the spa manager to make sure new recruits were informed of this important tidbit.

She found a spot at the railing and leaned against it, breathing in briny air. Down below on the sand, couples walked so close together that no light could seep between them. Truthfully, she was surrounded by happy people these days. Sophia and Christian had just returned from their honeymoon, their expressions reflecting their deeper connection. Meg and Jackson had overcome their troubles to create a beautiful family together. And Liddy and Beau, though she didn't know them as well as the others, glowed with love for each other every time she encountered them.

She was happy for all of them. Truly. And if Priscilla had learned anything during her trials, it was that she did not need a man to make her life complete ... although if one were to come along who looked at her the way all three of her new friends' husbands looked at them? Well. She wouldn't be opposed to that kind of thing.

She reached into her purse and pulled out a tube of hand gel infused with lavender essential oil and rubbed the healing concoction into her parched skin.

Eventually, hunger turned in her stomach, so Priscilla pushed away from the railing that skirted the path along the sea and headed for the restaurant. Most people choose not to stay at their place of employment for fun, but ever since she walked into Sea Glass Inn the year before to search for her old friend Meg, and perhaps get a glimpse of a mermaid, she'd been mesmerized by the place. If she could lease a suite to stay in full-time, she would.

"Hi Priscilla," Trace said. "Heard the newbie scalded you today. You should put some butter on that."

"That's not a bad idea." Priscilla held up her fingers for Trace to see. "For now, my hand gel is working quite well, but I'll try your antidote when I'm home."

"You're always so positive. That's what I like about you!" Trace shoved a fist into her side and cocked her chin toward the cafe. "If you're goin' into that restaurant, make sure they give you the employee discount. Otherwise there's no way you can afford that food on your hairdresser salary."

"Thank you for your sweet concern, Trace."

A wolf whistle rudely interrupted their banter.

Trace shook her head at Thomas, the inn's young-gun valet. "She's old enough to be your—"

"Older sister!" Priscilla said, laughing.

Priscilla made her way into the restaurant, more determined than ever to snag a table by the window overlooking the sea. Johnny, the bartender, winked at her as she strolled in. "You off the clock now?"

"You bet."

He grabbed a towel and rubbed it vigorously on the restaurant's shiny bar. "Something tells me you're going to be a lifer around here." His gaze lingered. "I mean that in a good way."

"Of course." She pointed to a seat where light from the setting sun poured in. "Mind if I grab that table by the window?"

"It's the last one—and it's yours."

"Grazie," she said, a holdover from her time in Italy. "And would you send over a spritz, please. The driest Prosecco you have, eh?"

"Sure thing, Doll."

She strolled to the window, took her seat, and exhaled once again, tightness flowing out of the muscles of her shoulders. Jenny, a server, deposited her drink onto her table and she picked it up, holding it listlessly.

"Can I get you anything else?" Jenny asked.

She glanced at the glass of Prosecco, remembering the evening *aperitivos* she experienced on her adventure through Italy—lovely in-between meals and drinks.

"Yes, thank you for asking. I think I would like to have your burrata appetizer."

"Absolutely. I'll bring that right over."

Priscilla took a sip of her wine and glanced out the window. An older couple moseyed over to where she had stood by herself earlier this evening. She rubbed her sore hand, thinking. Italy was beginning to seem like such a long time ago. She had run off to that glorious country, just as Meg had, to escape her problems and to find happiness again—and she'd met all kinds of precious people along the way.

And yet, why did she suddenly feel so all alone? She bit her own tongue. Enough of that nonsense. She had a new life and it was good. She took another sip of her drink.

Jenny delivered her appetizer and left her to enjoy the huge plate of burrata, tomatoes, and fresh baked bread. The presentation, the aroma ... the entire experience was like joy to the palate.

She first saw him out of the corner of her eye while savoring a fluffy bite of the cheese. He and Johnny were bantering about the Dodgers—although it was clear that he was more of an Angels fan.

Wade stood at the bar, alternating between looking at the screen behind Johnny and sneaking a peek at her. She hadn't seen him in a couple of weeks or so. In that time, she had not had a chance to drive out to the center, but she had received several calls from Amber. Though the young girl called with questions about hairstyles, Priscilla sensed a need in Amber's voice, one that wasn't limited to hair care.

The two men at the bar continued their discussion, their voices rising about stats and RBIs, bits of bravado pouring forth about which teams might make it to the World Series this year.

Baseball had been Leo's thing, too, and he had always taken it personally that the state of Virginia did not have its own major league team. Personally, she was grateful because, if truth be revealed, she found it a slow and rather uninteresting sport.

She yawned and tried to refocus her attention to the oceanscape outside her window.

"Are we boring you?" Johnny called from across the bar as he stacked glasses.

Priscilla smiled over at him and playacted another yawn, covering her mouth as she did.

Johnny threw back a husky laugh, the clink of glassware in the background.

Priscilla nibbled another morsel, laughter on her tongue. Wade had yet to say anything to her. How odd. Hadn't they spent enough time together to bypass the awkwardness and unfamiliarity that came along in relationships of the acquaintance variety?

Or maybe he thought she wanted something from him. Priscilla bit the inside of her cheek and tried to focus on the appetizer in front of her. What was this all about? she chided herself. She came here alone tonight to unwind, not because she was on the hunt for anyone. She was content, happy, even. Why in the world had Wade Prince's sudden presence—and seemingly detached stance—given her more than a single thought? She stared out the window, seeing nothing. *Chin up, girl. Chin up!*

When Priscilla took another bite of burrata and bread, she caught him glancing at her. Was he waiting for an invitation? Or disappointed that he'd ducked in here only to run into her again?

Johnny had disappeared to attend to a woman who had

taken a seat at the far end of the bar and the silence fell over the room like a stifling woolen blanket. Wade continued to stand at the bar, his side to her, ostensibly to watch the game.

She doubted that.

She leaned away from the window and sighed. "Are you going to join me or not?"

He pivoted. Slowly. Did she detect a deepening of color in his face? Like previously, Wade's gaze was noncommittal. "Didn't know I was invited."

Priscilla clucked her tongue and settled herself back in her chair.

He took a couple of steps forward, one hand in his pants pocket. "What?"

She shrugged. "I was thinking how very high school this conversation was, and I was about to say something to that effect."

"But?"

"But then I recalled a line from a movie, which said essentially 'high school was never over.'"

He moved closer now, that hand of his jiggling in his pocket. Unusual. He nodded to the chair across from her. "May I?"

She gestured for him to sit. "Please."

"You've been on my mind," he said.

She lifted her gaze to his. "Have I?"

"Yes. I spoke to my sister yesterday and—" he raked a hand through his thick hair— "you were right."

She scrutinized him. "How so?"

He sat forward, bringing her into a more intimate space. Regret clouded his eyes. "After my niece was born, my sister suffered from postpartum depression. I heard mention of it, of course, but had no idea how serious it could be."

Empathy tugged at her heart. "Was her case severe?"

"I don't really know. After you and I talked over coffee, I started to remember things—things I'd put out of my head." He flicked his wrist upward, as if surrendering. "I'd been working and traveling and as far as I knew, my sister was happy. She'd finally gotten the little girl she wanted—my niece, Sadie."

"And you figured everything was pink and perfect."

He nodded. "Yes, I really did. But in hindsight, she was suffering. She put on a happy face mostly, but if I'd been listening, I would have known something was wrong."

"Oh, Wade. I've never given birth, as you know, but I'm aware of the effect hormonal changes can make in a woman's psyche. You can't blame yourself for not understanding what is even difficult for us to understand." She sighed sympathetically. "It's likely that Gwynnie was hard-pressed at the time to explain what was going on inside of her."

He flipped a hard look at her. "Her ex-husband saw everything she was going through."

"And you think he took advantage?"

Wade's eyes hardened more, the effect like black marbles. "I know he did."

"I'm so sorry."

He drew in a harsh breath and let it back out like the luffing of a sail. "I love my sister, you know, and I love Sadie. Very much."

"I never doubted that."

He tapped his finger on the table. "I'm telling you, Priscilla —that little girl can have anything she wants. Anything. All she has to do is let her request leave those pretty little lips and it's hers."

Priscilla laughed softly, attempting to lighten the mood. "I would not recommend that she know about that for many years." When her laughter faded away, she said, "I'd love to meet her sometime. Does your sister come up this way often?"

"Not enough. I've been promising Sadie a swim in the hotel pool, though."

Priscilla gave him a sideways, questioning glance.

He leaned forward and tapped the tip of his pointer finger on the table again, the beginnings of a grin on his face. "Hey. I have an 'in' with the owners of this place."

"Well, then, you'd better make good on your promise."

The darkness began to clear from his expression. His eyes caught with hers now and they seemed to startle, as if seeing her in a new way. Or was she imagining that?

Wade licked his lips and Priscilla felt heat rising in her cheeks. Her lungs stilled, as if she couldn't quite get the breath she needed. She wanted to look away, and yet, wouldn't doing so draw attention to her response to him?

"I've made this all about me," he said simply.

"You had something heavy on your heart. No need to apologize for that."

His gaze did not waver. "Tell me more about you."

Again, her lungs constricted. She couldn't breathe. What did he want to know? What did she care to say? She blinked and darted a glance out the window. The sun had set, leaving behind a fuchsia sky.

"Priscilla?"

She turned back to face him. "What would you like to know?"

"I'd like to know how you are doing?"

"How I am doing ... what exactly do you mean?"

Wade leaned back, his shoulders lowering, as if relaxing. He continued to zero in on her, though, and it unnerved her, though she wasn't sure why. "You told me recently that your husband left you. Tell me about that."

She frowned. "There isn't more to tell. Truly."

"I apologize if it sounds like I am prying. But that had to be difficult. You listened to me, now I want to know how you are *really* doing."

First her eyelids began to blink. Almost as if on their own volition. A trickle of emotion began to work its way through her chest and up her neck, until reaching a floodgate that threatened to open. She blinked away the flood and cleared her throat, swallowing. "I'm—I'm doing quite well. Like I said, I am in a new place, with new friends—"

"And yet I find you here, having dinner alone."

She snapped a look at him. "I could say the same of you."

He nodded once, his lips pressed together lightly.

They sat in silence, staring at each other. Finally, she said, "Okay." Even though she started to speak, she found herself looking away, off into the sea's distance. When she swung her gaze back to Wade, the words nearly barreled out of her. "There were some in my circle of friends, my church, specifically, who questioned the divorce." She hadn't told that to anyone before.

He cocked his head to the side, as if assessing her. "You mean, whether you should have gone through with it?"

Those tears that always threatened to make their entrance when she thought about this element from her past did not change course now. She worked to hold them back.

"And that bothers you."

She nodded. "I love God. Very much. But sometimes his people, well, his people's words have the ability to sever the heart. Do you know what I mean?"

"I believe I do, but why don't you tell me."

She inhaled deeply. "There are some that said I should never marry again, that it would be against God's law, since I was married in the church. Not that I'm looking for a husband at the moment." She shrugged, failing to avoid eye contact with him. "Still, it wasn't something I thought I would hear from ... friends. Nor do I think their interpretation of the Bible—of God's opinion—was correct."

He gave her a smile that was one part awkward and ten parts kind, but said nothing.

She continued. "I've found that sometimes the people who should be there to help you through make healing the most difficult."

Shoving manners aside, Wade put his elbow on the table and leaned his face into his hand, thoughtfully. He held her eyes with his own. "So," he said, "you spent your time with Pharisees."

A grin broke across her face, though the fortress of tears behind her eyes had not waned. She didn't care to call anyone from her past names, and yet, by his words, she knew he understood.

He reached for her hand. "I'm sorry they hurt you."

She attempted to shake off his sympathies. "I'm fine. Truly. You-you just asked how I was doing and I, well, I had a moment of honesty." She laughed, albeit nervously now.

He continued to caress her hand with his, which, she noted in her haze of emotion, sent all kinds of electrical forces through her body. Unlike earlier, her skin felt no pain at all. She licked her lips, forced a bright smile on her face, and put off all thoughts of the past.

Then she leaned forward, turned her hand upward ever so slightly and looped her fingers around his.

CHAPTER 7

Priscilla stood in front of her floor-length mirror, scrutinizing the mesh cover-up she wore over her emerald green swimsuit. Because of her red hair and light skin, she'd always been told green was her color. But she had never bought into the cliché. Though she tried. She leaned her head to one side, gazing into that mirror, feeling more like a teenager than a forty-something woman.

She gasped, remembering that a certain teen had texted her an hour ago. Priscilla rifled through her tropical bag, stashed on her bed, and found her phone.

AMBER: *Can I come to the inn?*
Priscilla: *I will make it happen.*

PRISCILLA GLANCED UP, hoping the young girl wouldn't insist on naming a date just yet. First, she'd have to check her work schedule, and then she would have to call Candace to find out how to go about planning a field trip for a foster child. She would likely need to touch base with the girl's foster family—

AMBER: *My foster mom says I can go on Monday. Pick me up?*
   Amber again: *Ok with you? Please?*

SO MUCH FOR CAREFUL PLANNING. She'd check with the various authority figures anyway, but from the looks of things, there would be no problem. Priscilla logged into the app that held her work schedule. The app had been a recommendation Wade had made to Jackson to help alleviate frantic calls from employees who forgot to take their schedules home with them. As she expected, she was not scheduled on Monday. She opened iMessage on her phone.

PRISCILLA: *I'll pick you up at 10 am. Bring a swimsuit.*

MINUTES LATER PRISCILLA strolled toward Meg and Jackson's condo on the far end of the complex. They lived near each other, but the community was so large, and both Jackson and Meg worked so much, that she rarely bumped into them when home.

The soft clip of her heeled flip-flops resounded in her ears, anticipation rising. Meg had thrown together this little pool soiree on the fly, because that's what she did. No matter that she booked events for the inn—for a *living*. She still found the time, and the energy, to whip up a gathering of friends.

Priscilla's heart swelled at the thought that she was

counted among them. God's providence. That's what she'd always thought about her "chance" meeting with Meg, which eventually led her to this place, to this new life. She picked up the pace, anxious to be among friends. And if she were completely honest, she couldn't wait to see ... *him.*

Wade had been invited too, and he had asked to bring Sadie along so that her momma could have a spa day. How sweet was that? And even before he had known that Priscilla was among the invitees, he asked her to join them.

"May we pick you up?" he had asked.

She should have said yes. In fact, with each step, she questioned why she hadn't. Instead, she had said, "How about I meet you there?"

"Whatever you'd like." Wade's voice came through warm, a hint of a smile in it.

She reached Meg and Jackson's home, raised knuckles to knock, but the door swung open before she could. "Priscilla!" Liddy stood with a kiddo on her hip, her smile robust. She pulled Priscilla into a tight hug, squashing the child between them. When she let her go, she said, "Come in, come in. Meg's made some fabulous Sangria—I'm no longer nursing so I can join you in having a glass!"

As if on cue, Jackson showed up in the entryway with two glasses of red Sangria, orange slices floating on top. "Cheers, ladies." He handed them each a glass. "They're plastic, so you can take them out to the pool with you."

Liddy giggled and leaned sideways toward Priscilla. "Even at home he takes risk management seriously."

Meg dashed from the kitchen and planted a kiss on Priscilla's cheek. "So glad you're here! You should see the cake Chef sent over for us." She looked toward the heavens for a second, a serene smile on her face. "It's going to be sublime. You'll see."

Liddy cut in. "Get this: It's a rum-and-espresso-infused ladyfingers chocolate mousse cake. How can that even be legal?"

"I can't wait," Priscilla said, flush with anticipation.

A male voice interrupted their banter. "You mean, you can't wait to see us?"

At Wade's voice, all three women turned. The little girl in his arms had buried her nose and eyes in his neck, her brown ringlets covering most of her face.

"This is Sadie," he said, pride evident.

Meg dashed over and gave them both a squeeze, then kissed Sadie on the cheek with a loud "mwah."

"Aw, hi Sweetie," Liddy said, reaching out to rub the girl's arm, her voice coaxing.

Sadie lifted her head slightly and peered at Liddy.

"I'm taking Beau Jr. out to the pool," Liddy said. "Can you help me find it?"

Like magic, Sadie jerked away from Wade's neck. He put her down and she grabbed onto Liddy's hand. Liddy turned and winked at Priscilla as she and Beau Jr. led little Sadie out the slider door toward the gated pool area.

Wade reached for Priscilla's hand. "Hi."

She tilted her chin up and caught his gaze. "Hi, back."

Meg had gone back to the kitchen where a helper had been filling chip bowls and restocking ice. She came through the doorway, hands full, mouth open as if she were about to say something when she froze. Her gaze drifted down to Wade and Priscilla's hands entwined and a small smile curled on her face.

Priscilla released Wade's hand and handed her drink to

him. "Can I help you carry some things out?"

Meg shook her head, a quick smile on her face. "No, please. You're my guests. You two go on out to the pool and relax. I've got it all under control."

Thankfully, she kept her real thoughts to herself, although she did send Priscilla a goofy little wink when she and Wade passed by her.

At the pool, several new faces sat at the barbecue island talking to Jackson, who wore an apron and tended to a smorgasbord of grilling meats. June gloom had passed this day by and the sun had shown up, wearing its summer best.

Wade found two lounge chairs near the edge of the pool. He handed Priscilla back her wine glass and dropped two towels onto one of the chairs. She took a seat in the one next to his and slipped her sunglasses on.

"Uncle Wade!" Sadie held onto the edge of the pool, her round brown eyes peering at him beneath soaking wet chocolate-colored hair. Liddy hovered nearby, with Beau Jr. on her hip. He was covered from neck to knees in a rash guard and tiny board shorts.

"Come in the pool, Uncle Wade!" Sadie called out.

Priscilla lowered her glasses and looked at him over the top of them. He had surprised her again. Instead of perfectly pleated white tennis shorts, he was in blue-with-white-trim board shorts and a T-shirt that bragged about his attention to his workouts. His feet were shod with leather flip-flops—the one and only telltale sign of his net worth.

"Pleeeeease ..." Sadie giggled fiercely, her dimpled cheeks pronounced as she cajoled Wade to join her in the water.

Wade's hands were on his slim hips, his grin wide. "How can I resist you?" In one languid move, he whipped off his T-shirt and plopped it onto his lounge chair. She looked away, but not before noticing his tight abs and catching the outline of a tattoo of an anchor on his upper back when he turned.

He was, in a word ... beautiful. So maybe that was embellishment, but truly, Wade's sudden display had awoken some dormant part of Priscilla. Warmth oozed through her, but not from the sun overhead.

He landed in the pool with a splash, setting off a ripple of giggles from his young niece. When he emerged next to her, his nearly black hair tousled from water, Priscilla tried not to stare.

Meg plunked down on Wade's lounge, startling Priscilla. "He's a great guy. Here"—she offered her a plate of veggies and hummus—"I brought you something to keep your strength up."

"Do I look like I'm wilting?"

Meg cracked up and swung her legs up to the lounger. She set a baby monitor on a glass side table and relaxed back, with a sigh.

"Never mind." Priscilla tried to keep herself from smiling like a teen at a rock concert. "Don't answer that."

"I'm glad you're dating him," Meg said, quietly.

"Well, darling, that is not entirely accurate."

"Oh no? Looked pretty cozy to me. I don't suppose you hold hands with just any old stud you run across."

"Oh, but I do," Priscilla said with a poker face.

Meg squealed and leaned over toward Priscilla. "Liar."

Priscilla took it all in—the pool teeming with adults and children, including Wade, the savory smoke from the BBQ, the laughter punctuating the blissful summer day.

"I'm glad to see all you workaholics enjoying yourselves," she said, changing the subject. "Even though you and Jackson aren't getting that much rest."

"Don't worry about us. All this"—she swept a hand in front of her, indicating the people and pool area—"gives us energy. Even Jax seems to love the commotion of people, though he's sound asleep right now."

"I'm with Jax," Priscilla said with a laugh. "Seriously, though, work is part of living, but so is play."

The bleating of a calf, shrill and insistent, interrupted their reverie. Or maybe it was a baby's cry.

Meg swung her feet back to the ground. "Welp, that's my cue."

"Bring him to me," Priscilla said. "I'd love to hold him."

Meg's smile was warm, yet tender. "Of course. I'll feed and change him first so you will get him at his best."

"Come in the pool, Cilla!"

Priscilla turned to the little girl calling her name. Sadie was seated on Wade's shoulder, her feet kicking against him. Water dripped from the tips of her pretty little toes down Wade's firm chest. *Mercy ...*

A teasing smile played on Wade's face. "Wanna play chicken?"

She kicked off her flip-flops. "How about I sit here on the edge and watch you two play?"

Sadie's eyes lit up. "I know! You can watch Uncle Wade and me play Marco Polo!"

"Sounds perfect." Priscilla sat down on the concrete, her legs hanging over the edge. She swirled her freshly pedicured feet in the refreshing water.

"Watch us, Cilla!"

"Yeah, watch us, Cilla," Wade said, with a wink. He watched Sadie hopping around in the shallow end, then quickly ducked down beneath the surface of the water.

"I still see you, Uncle Wade," she said, scolding him.

Jackson appeared beside Priscilla. "Yeah, no cheating Uncle Prince!"

Sadie giggled at Jackson. "It's Uncle Wade, not prinz."

"My mistake," Jackson said good-naturedly. He plopped down next to Priscilla as Wade and Sadie continued their game of Marco Polo. "Enjoying yourself?"

"Very much so." She assessed him. "And, if you don't mind my saying, boss, I think having some time away from the inn is good for you."

"Is that so?"

"Well, look at you—you're tan, smiling, have fewer wrinkles—"

"Wrinkles?"

"The kind brought about from stress."

"And I look calmer now, do I? You know we have a baby in the house now, right?"

She laughed lightly. "He's keeping you young. And so is Meg, I suspect."

He whooped out a laugh. "I'm sure she would love to hear you say that." He whipped another look at her, this one feigning seriousness. "Don't."

"Don't what?" Meg said, Jax in her arms. "And I'd love to hear Priscilla say what?"

Jackson leaned his head back, laughter bellowing.

Priscilla hopped up from the edge of the pool and stood next to Meg. She reached out her arms. "May I?"

Meg carefully placed Jax into Priscilla's arms and took a seat on the edge of the pool next to her husband.

Priscilla drew in the baby's scent, the action bittersweet. He smelled of everything she loved and longed for.

Beau wandered over. "Is this the kids' section?"

Liddy called out, "No. This is!"

Seconds later a preteen boy proved her point by landing a cannonball next to her, one that Priscilla might have rated a ten, if this was a competition and she a judge. Likely on instinct, Liddy pulled Beau Jr. into a protective embrace.

Beau's stance shifted and he looked as if he were about to dive into the pool fully clothed. He put a hand on his hip. "Want me to switch with you?" He shaded his eyes with his other hand.

A smile lit up Liddy's face. "No, but you could join me."

The man nearly melted right there on the spot—Priscilla could see it in the softening of his expression. He turned to remove his shirt and put it on a nearby chair when he noticed her there, holding Meg and Jackson's son. "Let me get you a chair, Priscilla."

Beau pulled a high-back chair away from a table and put it down close to the edge of the pool. "There," he said. "You'll be more comfortable, I think."

"And be closer to the action, too. Thank you very much." She settled into the chair and adjusted Jax's blanket so that it kept him out of the sun.

Wade continued to play with Sadie, tossing her gently in the shallow end, eliciting squeals. Liddy and Beau cooed over their son, introducing him to the water, and Meg and Jackson flirted with each other at the edge of the pool. She tilted her face up toward the sun, resting in the warmth that emanated from Jax, and embracing gratitude. This life was a far improvement from the one she'd left. And she was grateful.

Her thoughts began to drift even more, like kelp floating away on the tide. *This* could be their real life, hers and Wade's. They could be with their child, around the pool, with friends around them. She drew in a refreshing breath and let it out slowly. Wade Prince had shown her another side of himself today. If only ...

A spray of water landed on her face. She sat up, blinking away her haze of longing.

"Hey, beautiful." Wade peered up at her from the edge of the pool where he leaned on folded arms. Jackson kicked water at him, but he didn't flinch.

"Hi, yourself." She adjusted Jax in her arms, vaguely aware of the approach of fatigue in her muscles.

"Want me to take him?" Meg asked.

Priscilla smiled, cinching the baby closer. "I'm so happy to hold him, Meg. May I continue?"

"Oh girl," Meg said, laughing. "Help yourself."

"You're a natural," Beau said.

Liddy shushed him and Beau gave her a look that said, *What did I say?*

"You're so sweet," Priscilla said to Beau. "I love children. In fact, that's why I've loved getting involved with Wade's ...." She caught herself before finishing the sentence.

Wade darted a look at her as her voice faded away. Her heart clenched. How could she have forgotten her promise to him to keep quiet about the center?

They exchanged a glance, powerful on its own, and instead of admonishment, she saw release. He pushed himself up on chiseled, warm brown arms and landed on his feet, water cascading down his form. He reached for a towel, tousled it over his hair, and draped it over his broad shoulders.

"Priscilla's already made a great impression at an education center for teens that I've been championing."

Jackson's forehead bunched, his eyes drawn together. "Is this some type of charity? Because I don't recall you mentioning it."

Wade's hands wrapped around the edges of the towel that he'd slung around his neck. "It is and that's because I haven't said anything"—he shrugged—"but it would be good for you to know."

Meg looked upward, shading her eyes. "Wow. This is the first I've heard of you doing something that isn't business related. I'm impressed."

Wade visibly scowled at this.

In response, Meg shook her head. "I didn't mean anything negative by that, Wade. You know we think the world of you! It's just that you're always so busy working that I'm surprised you have the time for something extracurricular."

"When you two take a break from running the inn, then we'll talk," Wade said, a bit of a smile back on his face.

From her spot in the pool, Liddy let out a snarky laugh. "He's got you there!"

Jackson cut in. "Whatever we can do to help, I hope you'll let us know."

Wade and Priscilla exchanged a glance. "I appreciate that."

Meg sprang up from her spot at the pool's edge. "Here, Priscilla, let me take him so you can cool off a bit."

Priscilla handed Jax back to his mother, then stretched out her arm and laughed. "I think it's creaking."

Wade unwrapped the towel from his neck and pretended to snap it at her. She gasped and shot him a look of horror. "What in the world?"

"Get in the water."

She laughed. "Or what?"

His grin was devilish.

Still smiling, she pulled a hair tie from her bag over on the lounge chair and rolled her hair into a messy bun. Then she unsnapped her cover-up, slipped it off, and draped it over the lounger. She turned back toward the pool and Wade stood there frozen.

"Ready?"

A slow smile, like a challenge, spread across his face. "Definitely."

∼

SHE'S GETTING *under my skin.*

They weren't safe in this pool together. Wade knew it in the core of his being, but did he suggest they climb out? That they retreat to separate corners of the pool?

Not a chance.

She swam toward him, that jolt of auburn hair perched precariously on top of her head. He imagined reaching up and undoing that hair tie ...

"You were right." She glided toward him, her voice husky. "The water feels amazing."

He nodded. She was cooling off. And he should too.

As luck would have it, though, they were unpredictably alone. Liddy had decided to take Beau Jr. in for a diaper change and a nap, and Sadie had insisted on joining her. "I can change poopy diapers," she'd proclaimed, although Liddy had assured her that there would be no need for that.

As she looked back, Sadie's tiny hand in hers, Liddy had assessed him with one long stroke of a knowing female glance. "I'm sure your Uncle Wade wouldn't mind that one bit."

He had almost laughed aloud. Either way, he'd made a mental note to pay her later.

Around the same time, young Jax had begun to squawk, sending Meg inside to care for him, and one of Meg's assistants cried out that the chicken could very well be burning and could Jackson come help?

Ah. They were blessedly, amazingly, incredibly ... alone.

"I hope you weren't too mad at me for blurting out something about the center." Priscilla pouted, the effect only heightening her charm. "I feel terrible about outing you without your permission."

He brushed his fingers across her lips and shook his head slowly, unable to help himself. "Ssh. I could never be angry with you."

Priscilla blinked rapidly, something he hadn't seen from her before. It took his breath away. Then she smiled. "I bet you could be."

He grinned and moved toward her, intimately aware of the closeness of their bodies, the occasional graze of his knees against hers, the gentle touch of her hands as she floated in the water. Though a warning sign flashed in his mind, he found himself barreling through the lights.

"Cilla," he whispered.

Her smile faded and he wondered if he had gone too far, had broken through the caution tape that was in place for a reason, and instead sent her dialing *911*. But as he took in her eyes, noting the way her pupils widened the longer he gazed at them, taking in her beauty, his misgivings drifted away.

"Wade," she said, the curve of her lips lovely, his sense of her heightened.

He moved closer, folding his hands into hers. In a flash, he was thankful they were out here in public, as he didn't dare do anything to cause mothers to shield their children's eyes. Not that he wasn't thinking about it ...

"You are a good man," she said.

He smiled, confused. "Why would you say that?"

She shrugged, smiling back at him, their hands still unashamedly entwined. "Because it's true. And I always say what is true."

He swallowed. Could he live up to her perception of him?

A sharp whistle interrupted the debate in his mind, pulling him dramatically to the present. He jerked a look toward the barbecue area. "Dinner's served," Jackson shouted, waving them over.

He let go of Priscilla's hands, and once she was free, she splashed him, and began swimming toward the shallow end. Wade pursued her until they reached the wall, dragged themselves out, and toweled off.

Later, after they'd eaten and laughed and talked until all the children were limp from exhaustion, Priscilla joined him on a walk to his car. Sadie was molded to his shoulder, occasionally letting out a snuffling snore. They reached his vehicle faster than he would have liked and his mind wound around a track, searching for something more to add to their quiet conversation.

"I bet her mama will be so happy to have Sadie back—and ready for bed, too." Priscilla stroked the young girl's hair as they stood there beneath a burgeoning sky.

He glanced upward. "So clear tonight."

She followed his gaze. "Yes. It is. No fog at all."

"If we stayed here long enough, I bet that big old sky up there would be full of stars."

She tipped her chin up toward him. "You do, do you?"

His gaze swept across her eyes, her mouth, that button nose of hers. "Maybe one of these clear nights we can go for a walk." He flicked his gaze westward. "Out there, on the beach."

She licked her lips, her eyes trained on him. "I would like that."

A sense of falling pressed itself up against his back and he tightened his grip on Sadie. He hadn't felt this way in ... well, had he ever? Had it been this way with Sophia? Suddenly, he couldn't remember a thing about that time.

"Will I see you at the inn this week?" she ventured.

He closed his eyes, reality a poor friend.

Priscilla flashed a smile, but he could tell by her body language, by the way she took an ever-so-slight step backward, that she had misinterpreted his response.

He reached for her arm with his free hand, pulling her back toward him. Her eyes, though downcast, flickered upward, apprehensive.

"I'm flying to New York in the morning."

She flashed a wider smile, though he noted the tension in her eyes. "Well, of course, darling. I'm sure you have much on your plate with your many businesses—"

He tipped his head until his forehead leaned against hers, still holding Sadie tightly against him with one arm. "Priscilla," he whispered. "I was going to say that I'm leaving for the City for a week, but I hope you won't mind a call from me when I return."

Those clear eyes of hers were on him again. She nodded and opened her mouth to answer him, but he stopped her, his lips finding hers with a kiss, soft yet tentative.

He pulled away, and as he did, Sadie stirred. She turned her face away from where it had been buried in Wade's neck, released a heavenly sigh, and collapsed back onto his shoulder.

Priscilla laughed lightly at that, her expression open, transparent. "I'd have to agree with you on that, dear one," she said to Sadie as she reached up and stroked the young girl's mop of dark curls. "Yes, I definitely agree."

CHAPTER 8

Yesterday played in her mind on a loop. It started with the vision of him, his strong hand holding his young niece's hand, and ended with that toe-curling kiss. Even now, as she walked into the lobby of the inn, her legs threatened to buckle under the power of that kiss's memory.

"Hey, Priscilla," Thomas called, as he jogged toward the valet lot, car keys in hand.

She waved in response and entered through the inn's double doors. Inside, the lobby buzzed. The sun had decided to come out today—always a reason for celebration on this part of California's coast, where fog showed up, bags in hand, without so much as a call first.

As proof of the sun's ability to wake up the central coast's inhabitants, Trace had a phone in her ear and a line of people waiting for assistance at the concierge desk. Trace wore her emotions on her sleeves, and if Priscilla had to guess what she was feeling right now, she'd say panic.

Priscilla checked the time on her phone and slipped

behind the counter, joining Trace. Amber's foster mother had decided to drive out to the inn to meet her and they weren't due in for another twenty minutes.

A platinum-haired woman in cute jeans and a knit top approached her. "Dear, could you tell me how to get to wine country? My friend and I would like to take a drive up there and visit some wineries."

"Yes, of course," Priscilla said, and abruptly turned when Trace started slapping her on the rotator cuff with a flyer. She took it and handed it over to the woman. "Here is a list of the wineries in the Los Olivos area, along with a map to get there."

The woman's friend peered over her shoulder. "That looks far."

"It's still early," Priscilla said, winging it. "Would you like me to see if there are spots left on a wine excursion?"

The first woman nodded. "I hadn't thought of that."

"Then we could drink all the wine we want," the friend quipped.

Priscilla laughed. "That is certainly true."

Trace hung up the phone with a dramatic flair and let out a groan. She exhaled and pushed Priscilla aside in a way that was neither mean-spirited nor apologetic. "Here, let me help you with that. You like red or white best?"

The platinum-haired woman frowned. "I don't understand."

Her friend cackled. "She's talking about wine. And we like it all, so give us your best tour."

"Okay, ladies. You sit right over there"—she used the flyer to point toward the comfy overstuffed couches that flanked the lobby fireplace—"and I'll get crackin' on this."

The phone rang and Trace quirked a look at Priscilla. "You going to get that?"

Priscilla startled and reached for the handset. "Sea Glass Inn, concierge desk."

"Priscilla?" Wade's voice, deep and professional, came through the line.

"Wade."

He laughed, the sound of it like warm butter to her hungry soul. "This is ... unexpected," he said. "Have you taken a new position at the inn?"

"Not at all. I came in to wait for Amber and noticed a line at the concierge desk."

He whistled. "So you jumped in to help. Is there anything you can't do?"

"Stop," she chided him, turning away from Trace. "Is there something I can help you with?"

"Forget about that. Then again, yes, there is something you can help me with, Ms. Cornwall. You can have dinner with me when I return from New York."

The warmth of a blush crept up her neck. "Sounds lovely."

Trace spun around, her brows kitted together tightly. "What sounds lovely?"

Priscilla put her hand over the phone and mouthed, "It's Wade."

"Mm-hmm. I see. Well tell him we've got work to do."

Priscilla licked her bottom lip. Should she remind Trace that she didn't actually work at the concierge desk?

Wade interrupted her thoughts. "It's a date then."

She nodded, though he couldn't see her. "It is."

The lobby doors opened and Amber came bounding in, more animated than she had ever seen her. Beside her was a squat woman in workout clothes, her long, black hair pulled up into a thick ponytail. The woman jostled her keys in her hand and swiveled her chin back and forth, as if looking for someone.

"Wade?" she said, her eyes trained on her guests, "Amber's here."

"And you have to go." He sounded almost ... sad.

She bit her bottom lip now, trying to squelch a smile that almost certainly showed up on her face. His voice was like cream added to a smooth espresso. How had she not noticed that before?

"I'll see you when you get back." She wanted to tell him to be safe, to get a good night's sleep, and to have a good time—but not too good, so he'd want to return. But instead, all she added was, "Bye for now."

Amber and her foster mom approached the desk. "This where you work?" the girl said.

Priscilla shook her head, slung her bag over her shoulder, and came around the front of the desk area. "I was using the phone." She reached out her hand to Amber's foster mom. "I'm Priscilla."

"Cilla," Amber reminded her.

Priscilla laughed. "That's right. The girls have given me a nickname."

The woman pumped her hand once and let it go. "I'm Lynn. Can I see some ID?"

"Lynnnnn!" Amber whined.

Priscilla smiled and pulled her bag open. "I don't mind, Amber. We all want to make sure you are in safe hands." As she held out her driver's license, she flipped a look at Lynn. The woman's stern expression appeared the norm, as if her frown was as comfortable as a well-worn shoe.

"That looks fine," Lynn said. She turned to Amber, her

expression less harsh. "You be good. Listen to Miss Cornwall, you hear?" Then she looked back to Priscilla. "You'll drive her back home?"

"Absolutely."

When she'd gone, Priscilla put her arm around Amber, ushering her toward the cafe.

"Where we goin'?" Amber asked.

"Was thinking of having a stack of pancakes. How does that sound?"

"You eat carbs?"

Priscilla grinned. "With pleasure!"

They took a table on the patio where the sun beamed, the air punctuated by the inn's population awakening to the call of seagulls and the ongoing splash of low-lofting waves. It was the perfect kind of day for what she had planned and she tilted her chin to the sky, sending God a quiet thank you.

After two stacks of pancakes, a bowl of fruit, and two glasses of juice were delivered, they both dug in.

"Lynn was kinda mad," Amber finally said.

Priscilla froze. "About bringing you here? Oh darling, I would have gladly driven out to pick you up."

"Nah. Wasn't that. She's just ticked she has to live so far inland." She shrugged. "Says it's hot and dusty. I think she wanted to drive me so she could go to the beach."

"Oh?"

Amber nodded. "Yeah, I saw a beach chair in the trunk."

"Sounds like you come out to the beach often."

"Never." She dug back into her stack of pancakes with gusto, dipping each forkful into a moat full of maple syrup.

"I see. Well, did you bring your swimsuit?"

Amber's expression fell, the corners of her mouth tugging downward. A tear fell onto her hand and instinctively Pricilla reached out and grasped it. "Oh, don't cry. If you forgot your suit, it's no problem."

The teen pulled her hand away, wiping her eyes with the back of her hand. "I figured shorts were good enough."

"Or we could visit the inn's gift shop. My treat."

Amber frowned. "Isn't that for old ladies?" Her expression showed that she was dead serious.

Priscilla collapsed against the back of her chair, laughing. She hadn't been a teen in, um, too many years. What did she know about what they liked to wear? As she thought about it, she realized there were an awful lot of floral prints in that gift shop—she'd have to discuss that with Meg one of these days. She leaned forward. "Maybe you're right. There's a cute shop I've been meaning to check out over at the harbor. We'll go there first. Sound good?"

Amber shrugged a shoulder, but her countenance softened. She continued scooping up pancake bites with gusto as Priscilla's gaze drifted out to the lively path of visitors heading down to the beach. Her mind drifted back to Jackson and Meg's party and the way she had reacted to Wade—and he to her. In the past couple of days, the daydream had showed up like a fairy godmother who'd stitched a broken heart and disappeared with a poof only to reappear and do it all over again.

When their plates were empty, Priscilla stood. "Let's go! We have a whole day to conquer."

"You have way more energy than other people your age," Amber said, following along.

She looked at the girl over her shoulder. "How old do you think I am anyway?"

Amber shrugged, a tiny smile on her lips. "Fifty or something?"

Priscilla gasped. "Darling, when I am fifty, I will embrace my life just as I do now, but dear girl, I am not yet there. Not for a long while."

"Whatever."

And there it was, the word that every teen seems to have in their repertoire so they could whip it out at precisely the right moment.

They rounded the corner into one of the newly designed halls that served as a type of gallery for sketches by Sophia. A fashion designer by trade, she leant her talents to the inn that she and Jackson own.

Amber slowed, her gaze curious, jumping from drawing to drawing until settling on one. "Who did these?" she asked.

Priscilla stopped in front of the one that had caught Amber's eye. It was of a girl in a long white coat with bold black buttons. She stood near the edge of the railway, her hair drifting away from her head, as if on a breeze. Very cosmopolitan, yet fun, too.

"Hello, Priscilla."

Priscilla stepped back quickly, startled. "Sophia! How lovely to see you." She glanced at Amber. "We were just admiring your work."

Sophia gave her a kind smile, her humility evident. She looked Amber in the eyes and reached out a hand. "Hello, I'm Sophia."

"This is my friend, Amber," Priscilla said.

Amber shook her hand, staring up at her. "You drew the pictures?"

"I did."

"Wow. They're really good."

"Why thank you, Amber. Do you like to draw?"

Amber shrugged, a gesture she'd shown more than once

when confronted with a question she either didn't want to answer—or didn't know how to.

"Well," Sophia said, unfazed, "you have your life ahead of you. Many years to discover what you love to do the most."

Sophia turned to Priscilla. "I was wondering if you have seen Wade today? I need to speak with him about a matter as soon as possible."

Priscilla's mind went suddenly where it should not have. Sophia was a married woman—a happily married one. Then why did her question prick the balloon that had been holding her heart aloft for days, sending it into a gradual spiral?

"I, uh, actually, I believe he's on his way to New York right about now."

"Oh." Even when she was disappointed, Sophia was beautiful. "Well then, perhaps I'll try to phone him."

Priscilla nodded. "Yes, yes, that would be best."

When Sophia had gone and she and Amber were in Priscilla's car on the way to the harbor bikini shop, Amber said, "Cilla? Why don't you like Sophia?"

Priscilla shrank back, still holding onto the steering wheel. "I love Sophia! Why would you think that I don't like her?"

Amber was doing that shruggy thing again. "You were giving off vibes."

"I was not giving off ... vibes." She paused. "What kind of vibes?"

"Like you were protecting your stuff."

Priscilla's heart sank. She continued down the windy road to the harbor, but took a quick glance at her teenaged passenger, seeing her in a blindingly new light. How many times had this poor girl moved taking everything she owned with her? How often had she found herself "protecting her stuff"? A knot formed in her throat. If Amber saw in Priscilla what she said she did, then it must have been there. Because she would know.

They pulled into a space in the parking lot that abutted the concrete path surrounding the harbor where boats of varying sizes were moored. A man in a pirate getup strolled along, an eye patch over one eye and a parrot on his shoulder.

"That looks crazy," Amber said. She turned toward Priscilla. "Can we go see him?"

Priscilla smiled, grateful for a change of subject.

Together they wandered down to the water's edge, stopping long enough for Amber to feed the parrot. Afterward, they walked over to the ice cream place with the line out the door and Priscilla made a mental note not to worry about the calories, but instead, to revel in the moment. The sun was overhead, she was with a new friend, and they had a day of adventures, whatever they may be, ahead of them.

"Psst, look over there," Amber said, before taking another lick of her chocolate brownie ice cream.

Priscilla tilted her head. "At the older couple?"

"Yeah." She took another nibble of her ice cream. "Aren't they cute, sharing that ice cream like that?"

She was right. The two were sitting next to each other at a small, round table with one cup of ice cream and two spoons. Priscilla smiled. "They are darling."

Amber gave her an impish smile, and inhaled the rest of her cone.

By the time they found the bikini shop, they had already feasted on a stack of buttermilk carbs and an ice cream chaser, giving them both more energy than if they had downed two espressos. Amber's eyes grew saucer-wide at the abundance of swimwear and cover-ups hung floor to ceiling in the small shop. And by the looks of the clientele, Priscilla knew they'd hit the jackpot. She was definitely the matron of the bunch.

That suited her fine. She joined the throng on the hunt, the scrape of hangers against long metal racks ringing in their ears. Calls of "look at this" and "this is perfect" and "do you have this in blue?" punctuated the air like corn popping under a heat lamp.

She had forgotten how exhilarating shopping could be.

And downright frustrating too ...

"I look so fat in this." Amber peered into the mirror after she'd tried on her fourth pair of bikini bottoms.

Priscilla had already learned it was fruitless to tell her how beautiful her body was and how lovely she looked. Saying so would somehow drive the stake of criticism further into her heart. Just when she began to wonder if they would ever make it to the beach, the shop owner stuck her head into the room.

"Don't mind me." She held out a pair of board shorts with swirls of dark chocolate and baby blue on them. "I thought you might want to try these—they're a favorite around here. And the great thing is, you can pair them with any bikini top you like." She handed Amber the shorts. "Ta ta, ladies!"

Amber's eyes lit for the first time since she began trying on swimsuits.

"Try them on," Priscilla said, trying not to look overly excited. She didn't care to ruin the moment with too much enthusiasm.

Amber swiveled once in front of the mirror. "These are perrrrffffect!"

"I agree." She hoped her words of positive affirmation would not somehow change Amber's mind.

Minutes later, they exited the shop and Amber said, "Whatdya want to do next?"

Priscilla slowed. She looked out to the harbor where several paddle boarders rowed along, like synchronized swimmers. She raised an eyebrow at Amber. "Want to try it?"

"Getting on one of those surfboard things?"

"Sure. Why not?"

Amber shrugged, but this time the action was accompanied by a huge smile. "Heck, yeah."

~

She had not laughed this much in months. After driving back to the inn and shimmying into their swimsuits, Priscilla and Amber walked down to the Kayak Shack to rent paddle boards. A guy named Brett gave them a ten-minute lesson on how to start out on the board—and released them out into the harbor as if they knew what they were doing.

Amber had amazing balance. While Priscilla had to begin by paddling out on her knees, Amber stood up from the get-go, feet shoulder-length apart on the grip pad, her shoulders erect and relaxed.

"C'mon, Cilla," Amber coaxed as Priscilla paddled out into the middle of a channel. "You can do it. I know you can stand."

She peered over her shoulder at the young girl. "You make it look easy!"

Amber laughed, digging her paddle into the water left side, right side, left side ... "It's super easy! My dog could do it ... well, if I had a dog, he could do it. Try to get up, okay? It's funner that way."

Priscilla's board wobbled more than she had hoped, the wake of a nearby boat wreaking havoc with her balance. She thought back on her conversation with Wade, remembering how he preferred "sides" on his water-going vessels. At this moment, as seawater splashed over her board, she began to see his point.

"Do it, Cilla!" Amber coaxed, obviously reveling in her ability to master paddle boarding in such a quick minute.

"Alright, yes, here I go."

"Yeah, here you go."

Priscilla laughed, almost to tears, but she held herself steady landing one foot on the grip pad, then the other. Slowly she stood, holding the paddle out to one side and her other arm out to the other for balance. She reminded herself to breathe.

"You did it! Woot—yeah, girl!"

Amber was enjoying herself, and to Priscilla, that alone was worth the price of admission, aka the demise of her ego.

"Let's go out to the main channel!" Amber shouted as her paddle picked up speed.

"Whoa, hon! Let me get acclimated, okay?"

Amber sighed good-naturedly. "Fine. I'll do donuts around you."

"Ha, ha, ha."

For the next fifteen minutes, Priscilla practiced paddling and balancing and basically trying not to die or seriously injure herself while Amber paddled in a zig-zag pattern, investigating docks and rigs moored on them. Once she found her rhythm, Priscilla noticed something especially addicting: calm. No phone, no noise—ambient or otherwise, just the peaceful bounce of the sea and air. She drew in a long breath of crystal air and allowed it to fill her completely from the inside out.

Amber floated up next to her. "This is the best day ever," she said, simply.

"Tell me why."

"I dunno. Maybe cuz there's no drama."

"You mean, because the water is calm."

Amber puffed out her lips, thinking. "I like getting to do this by myself. Well, with you, I mean, but by myself too." She stuck her paddle into the water, giving it a small shove.

Priscilla wondered more about Amber's life. How long had she been in foster care? Had she ever stayed in one place long enough to have bonded with anyone? Had she ever had her own room or did she always share?

Amber shot a glance over her shoulder, interrupting Priscilla's musings. "Race ya to the main channel!"

Priscilla grinned. "You're on."

Two hours later, they returned their paddle boards and showered off under the open-air spigot near the rental company.

"I'm starving," Amber said.

"Me too. There's a burger place close by. Does that sound good to you?"

Amber nodded, and five minutes later they were sitting on a wooden deck, waiting for their burgers while watching other newbies take out paddle boards.

Amber snorted a laugh. "That guy over there looks like you."

Priscilla cocked her head and looked toward a guy who was obviously going out for his first time. "What are you saying?"

"Just look at him. He's on his knees but looks all wobbly." She caught eyes with Priscilla. "Like you."

"Well, I'm insulted."

Amber bobbed her head and laughed, and Priscilla loved the look of it. Even if her ego had to take more hits to achieve such merriment.

They received their cheeseburgers and immediately set out to devour them. After a few bites, Priscilla set her burger down and considered Amber, who continued to eat with gusto.

"Amber, are you comfortable telling me about your living situation?" Priscilla asked.

Amber kept her eyes focused on lunch, a small shrug the only indication that she had heard Priscilla's question.

"If you're not, that's fine too. But if you'd ever like to talk about things, I want you to know that I'm here. And I'm a good listener."

Amber put down her food and wiped her mouth with the back of her hand. She gave Priscilla a brief, hooded look before glancing away toward the water. "Lynn's okay. She has little kids and no husband, so I try to help out around the house. It's okay."

"That's good of you to help."

"Whatever."

Priscilla watched a mask slowly materialize over Amber's face, one that attempted to hide any semblance of emotion from her expression. "And do you get along well with her children?"

"They're babies, but yeah, they're okay." She snapped a look up. "It's not like I'll be with them that long anyway."

"Why do you say that?"

"Cuz people don't adopt old kids like me." Her expression, which had begun closing off minutes ago, had almost completely shut down. She looked up, her eyes dull. "I'm a lifer."

A lifer?

Where had she heard that recently? A picture of Johnny, the inn's evening bartender, popped Priscilla's mind. He had said that about her one night, and it had been like a balm to her ears. It was as if he confirmed what she had already known—that she had come home. For life.

Priscilla took a hard look at Amber. The young girl was a chameleon of sorts. At EduCenter she could collapse into giggles with her friends on cue, but she could also shut down as quickly as she had with Priscilla right now. Her eyes grazed the young girl's face, compassion overwhelming her. While Johnny's pronouncement had given Priscilla a sense of peace, Amber's sounded more like a sentence, one that she had resigned herself to living.

Tears welled in Priscilla's eyes, but she blinked them away. Changing the subject, she said, "You had amazing balance out there. Have you surfed before?"

"Nah. Never been surfing. One time I was at the public pool though and my swimming teacher said I had good balance when I was learning how to go off the diving board. Maybe she wanted to make me feel good, but"—she shrugged—"maybe I kinda do."

"Well, I was impressed."

"You should be. I thought you were gonna fall off!"

"Good thing I didn't."

"Yeah." Amber giggled. "I didn't want to have to go into that icky water and save you."

"But you would've?"

She shrugged. "Guess so."

CHAPTER 9

Katrina leaned close to Priscilla, a tinge of guilt in her voice. "Just one more? Pretty please?"

Priscilla was flat ironing a client's hair, supposedly her last client of the day. A very long day. But she couldn't say no to Katrina.

At her nod, Katrina gave her a weird little side hug and scampered off. Her client, a guest in the hotel, smiled at her in the mirror. "You're an angel," the woman, who looked to be in her fifties, said. "You've been on your feet since the minute I walked in here two hours ago to get my pedicure. Wish I had your energy!"

Priscilla chuckled. "What can I say? I love my job." She set the flat iron down on the counter and put her hands on the back of the woman's chair. Looking at her in the mirror, she asked, "What do you think?"

The woman clapped her hands together and let out a squeal. "I absolutely love it! I haven't looked this young in years. Priscilla, you are more than an angel—you're a magician."

"I'm so glad you like it!" She smoothed her hands over the woman's hair, shaping it around her face. She couldn't help herself. "If you have some dry shampoo with you, it should last you a few days."

"I do have some! Oh, thank you so much."

After the woman had gone on her way, Priscilla grabbed a broom and began sweeping under her chair. Katrina sidled up next to her. "I come bearing a gift," she said, holding up a pair of the inn's complementary slippers.

Priscilla laughed. "What this?"

"I really appreciate you staying a little later tonight and thought maybe your feet could use a break." She pointed to Priscilla's high-heeled sandals. "I have no idea how you stand on those every day."

Priscilla dumped a dustpan full of hair into a bin. She put away her broom and took the plastic-wrapped, terry cloth slippers from Katrina. "I'll admit—these do look perfect right about now."

She stepped out of her sandals and put them in the corner, then she slid her aching toes into the slippers. "Ahhh."

Katrina laughed. "Don't get too relaxed—your next client is here."

The woman looked about forty. She had a dimple in her cheek when she smiled, and wavy dark brown locks. Something about her seemed familiar, and Priscilla mentally scanned her mind, wondering if they had met before.

"Welcome." She motioned for the woman to sit in her chair. "I'm Priscilla."

"Hello, Priscilla. I'm Gwynnie."

Priscilla snapped a look up, meeting the woman's gaze in the mirror. The woman smiled back at her. "Wade's sister."

"Of course!" Priscilla nodded. "I see the resemblance between you and Sadie now. She is so darling."

"She has talked non-stop about you since the pool party. You made quite the impression on her," Gwynnie said.

Priscilla tilted her head to the side and splayed the fingers of one hand across her chest. "Really? That makes me so happy."

Gwynnie smiled, but didn't say anything more. Priscilla wracked her brain, trying to recall whether Wade had told her to expect his sister in the salon. Hadn't she already spent time at the spa on the day he had brought Sadie to the pool party?

"So," Priscilla asked, "what are we doing today?"

"I thought it would be fun to get to know the woman who has caught my brother's attention."

Priscilla froze. She wasn't aware that anyone else knew that she and Wade were, um, that they were maybe getting to know each other ...

Gwynnie flat out laughed. "I'm guessing I surprised you, didn't I?"

"Well, I ..."

"My brother and I are totally different. He's pretty stoic, at least about his personal life. Not me. I usually say what I think, not too worried about using a filter. Does that bother you?"

"Not in the least, honey. Makes it easier to get to know you."

"That's what I always say, too!"

Priscilla laughed. "Shall we get started?"

"Yes, please. And do whatever you want—I hear you are amazing."

"Who's telling you those lies?"

"Ha ha. I was in here last week getting a pedicure—well,

you know that already—when I overheard it. Then Wade mentioned his friend Priscilla, so I put two and two together and decided to stop in on my way through town to see if you could squeeze me in."

"I'm glad you did." She whipped out a cape and draped it over Gwynnie, latching it at the back of her neck. "Let's get you washed."

A few minutes later, Priscilla was running a wet brush through Wade's sister's hair and wondering how much she ought to share—and how much to keep to herself. "You know, Sadie seemed pretty smitten with her uncle. It was beautiful to see."

"Uncle Wade spoils her. I'd complain, but she needs a good male role model in her life, so I let him get away with it." She took a breath. "I know he told you about my ex."

When Priscilla hesitated, she added, "Because of you, my brother and I have reconciled. Not that we were estranged, but you said something that caused him to talk to me and hear my side of things." She turned slightly. "I really appreciate that."

Priscilla positioned strands of Gwynnie's hair between her fingers, ready to start snipping. "I'm glad you didn't mind me adding my two cents to your situation. He had expressed concern, so I simply said that there could have been more to the story than what he seemed to think."

"Whoo—you are so diplomatic."

Priscilla smiled.

"I really hope things work out between you two."

Priscilla kept her voice even. "We are really just beginning to get to know each other."

"Yes, well, my brother is a great catch, but he's also a workaholic. I'm sure this is no surprise to you."

Priscilla nodded. She continued to slide her fingers down sections of Gwynnie's hair, focusing on precision to the best of her ability.

She sighed. "Our father was a good man. Mom died when we were young so Dad buried himself in his pursuits. He was a funny man, but not that great at keeping money all the time. Some things made him a lot of money—like the little house he invested in that the state bought to make way for a highway. But then he'd reinvest and lose, not just a little of it, but *all* of it. Then he would start all over again."

"That must have been hard on you."

"Not really. I was too young to notice what was happening, but I learned when I grew older that my brother worried all the time. I don't think the yo-yo financial situation was such a great experience for Wade."

Priscilla didn't mention what Wade had divulged regarding his own financial status. "Is it possible that Wade actually learned much from your father about business?"

"Yes and no. I think he did pick up some pointers, whether he'd acknowledge that or not, but he also learned to be afraid. A hoarder, even." Gwynnie's eyes flashed wide in the mirror, as if she'd suddenly had a revelation. "I shouldn't have said that. Please don't judge my brother by what I've said. Promise me!"

"Oh, honey, you don't have to worry about that with me."

This appeared to calm her some. "I hope not. Wade's a good man. A little hyper-focused at times, but he's got a generous heart."

Priscilla nodded, thinking of the way Wade offered his time to the kids at EduCenter. He also didn't think twice about donating money—lots of it—when he learned of the need. Sure, she had seen signs of his grumpiness, but maybe she needed to cut the man some slack. Her mind fluttered back to the kiss he had surprised her with the other evening and realized, maybe she already had.

∽

Priscilla opened the shutters of her condo, ushering in the pinprick of light forcing its way through the fog. She, for one, was getting tired of the lack of sun.

Her cellphone rang. Someone was calling from EduCenter.

"Hello?"

"Priscilla? This is Candace James, from the center. How are you today?"

"Candace—how nice to hear from you. I'm doing very well, thank you."

Candace lowered her voice. "Listen, I wanted to tell you about a little situation, but I'd like you to keep it on the down low. Can you do that for me?"

Priscilla curled up on her sofa, curious. "Of course. Whatever you need."

"It's about Amber."

She sat up. "Is everything okay with her?"

"No. Not really. She had a disagreement with her foster mom and was kicked out."

"Kicked out? Oh, no. Where is she?"

Candace sighed. "I took her in on an emergency basis. I-I just couldn't let her be thrown back into the system again. She's a great kid, but she hasn't been able to develop much trust in other humans."

A knot formed in Priscilla's throat and she swallowed it back. "What can I do to help?"

"I'm so glad you asked, because, honestly, I was hoping that you would consider becoming her foster mother, Priscilla. I have never seen her take to someone the way she does to you. There's already a remarkable level of trust between you two."

Priscilla let Candace's words settle into her mind and heart. Instinctively, she knew the center's director was right—something special had developed between them. But become a foster mother?

"I know it's a lot to ask, and of course, you can say no. But I hope you'll think about it. She's going to be heading into high school soon and I shudder to think how she'll handle the pressure of all that without a stable home life."

Candace's words weighed on her and her mind whirred. Raise a teenager? That would be an unprecedented adventure, even for her who had traveled the world with only two pairs of shoes.

"Are you still there?"

Priscilla nodded. "Yes, yes. I am thinking about your proposition." She wondered what Wade might say. She hadn't been able to forget the way he kissed her the other night, the way he'd lingered with her out in the parking lot. Just about everything from that day had been so unexpected.

Like this phone call.

"I must warn you, though, that approval doesn't happen overnight," Candace said. "You'll have to apply and take a course. Then they'll have to inspect your home." She paused. "As board chairman, Wade could formally recommend you as well."

"I understand," she said. "And I am honored you would think of me. I promise to think seriously about this and get back to you as soon as possible."

"That's all that I ask."

CHAPTER 10

It had been a long week, but not without its perks. New York had always been a temptation for Wade, ever since his grandfather had taken him to the City when he was a kid—the first place he had been allowed to stay out until well after dark. He remembered pizza slices as big as his head, roving cartoon characters in Times Square, and strangely, jumping over the hot stench of subway exhaust as it bellowed out of the sidewalks.

The satisfaction of a job well done settled in his middle. He looked again at the signed contract on his iPad, the one that he had negotiated with his partners until well into last night. They had run into trouble several times, the deal nearly washed away, but in those times his heart pumped harder and his energy surged. Heavy hitters owned most of the block where his building, a large multi-unit structure he had invested in twenty years before with a group of partners, stood south of the garment district. Who knew that the rest of the block, except one old house, would be snatched up and plans made for a high-rise building that would stretch from corner to corner?

The building he owned sat squarely in the center of the block, a pre-war building that wore scars from the past. Buying into it had been a risk for him, especially back when his investing skills were raw and untested. But as of last night, that risk had paid off handsomely. The developer would have to purchase his investment property to build what had been proposed and approved by the city. And they had sweetened the deal by including future rental income losses in the final price.

Now all he and his partners had to do was wait for the owner of the final, small home next to theirs to be released to the developer. They had been assured that the small home was no *Up* story. The structure was not some memories-filled home that the current owner had lived in with a beloved wife. Instead, it had been passed down from a grandparent, had subsequently been rented out for many years, and desperately needed repairs.

He could not have asked for a better situation to find himself in.

Wade blew out a breath and settled into this high-backed first class seat, the rumble of the jet's engine a soothing tradition. The next time he flew to New York, it would be for fun. Maybe to see a show. Or tour MOMA again. As he considered his options, his eyelids began to feel heavy and the next thing he knew, they had landed at Los Angeles International Airport. He awoke to the sounds of seatbelt unclicking and bell tones alerting flight attendants that they would be disembarking soon.

Remarkably, he had slept through the entire flight. An inkling told him that the newly signed sales contract had something to do with that—and, perhaps, the fact that he had something—or someone—to look forward to seeing soon.

He exited the plane and searched out a restroom before heading for a place to grab some coffee. As he waited in line, he switched his phone on and watched it light up with texts like a gambling machine in Vegas. He frowned. He'd received two texts from Jackson asking when he would be back in town and a handful from EduCenter.

A new message popped onto his screen from Jackson:

EMERGENCY ISSUE *at board meeting tonight. If you are available, have a question.*

HE GRABBED HIS CAPPUCCINO, instantly wishing he had ordered two shots, and headed for the baggage area. His driver met him there and took his bag from him. He had traveled often enough to learn the art of traveling light. No checked bags for him.

He headed for the inn before going home, still buoyed by the caffeine and solid sleep he'd managed to get on the plane. He hoped this energy would last long into the night. Despite his wealth, the idea of spending such ludicrous prices for a seat on an airplane still made him bristle. But then again, would he have been this rested in coach?

An hour and a half later, Wade strolled into the inn, hoping to catch Jackson before his meeting began. He stifled a yawn, eager to continue moving forward as if he hadn't just flown across the country. He and Jackson had traded a couple of texts on the drive, but they were too brief to solve the issue at hand. As he turned the corner, he nearly ran into Priscilla.

"You're ... home," she said, her eyes bright.

He smiled at her. "Landed an hour ago and drove straight here."

She tilted her head the way he had begun to recognize. "Darling, do you ever sleep?"

"As a matter of fact, I caught some winks on the plane. How about you?"

"Do I ever ... sleep?"

Her question sizzled in his mind, taking him down roads he wasn't sure he should attempt to roam just yet. He measured his response, his tongue making a quick swipe across his bottom lip. "I meant, how are you? Are you off work now?"

She brushed a tendril aside with a swipe of her hand. "Yes, my shift just ended, and phew, it was a long one."

His gaze took her in—auburn hair cascading down her shoulders, eyes that sparkled, lips that tempted him ... *Pull yourself together, man.* "You look like you weathered it beautifully."

A voice from behind caught their attention. "Wade?"

He turned. Sophia had come up behind him, her smile tentative. He hadn't seen her in—how long?—since the wedding, probably.

"Sophia," he said. "I heard you were traveling."

"Yes, but it is good to be home. Hello, Priscilla."

Everything about her shouted contentment. She always did have a serene quality to her. At times he began to believe that her calm demeanor had been what had drawn him to her in the first place.

The three of them stood awkwardly in the hall, Wade sensing the urgency of Jackson's call. Did Sophia know what it was about? Or would it be news to her? He knew better than to divulge anything without knowing the answer to those questions. At the same time, he longed to spend time with Priscilla, to know how her week went. How had she spent it? Did her time with Amber go well?

Between the myriad questions and the sudden onset of travel fatigue—something he thought he had skillfully avoided—Wade experienced an uncharacteristic loss for words.

"Will you be joining our meeting this evening?" Sophia asked him.

The meeting. Yes. That's why he was there. His eyes felt jumpy. "Yes," he said. "I'm on my way there now."

"Wonderful. Can we walk together?"

He nodded and made a move forward. Then stopped, and pivoted, remembering Priscilla. "We weren't finished talking," he began.

Priscilla's bright smile told him she hadn't noticed his carelessness. "You go on ahead. I was heading home anyway." She paused, that smile unwavering. "Time to step out of these heels."

Don't tempt me, woman ...

"I'll call you," he said, almost completely flummoxed. Hurriedly, he bent and kissed her cheek. Then he watched her walk away.

When he turned around again, Sophia was waiting for him. She gave him a kind smile and they made their way down the hall and around the corner to the meeting room where Jackson and several advisors looked to be in a heated conversation.

An hour later, his mind and body spent, Wade retrieved his bags from the bell desk and strode out of the lobby doors. The valet on duty hailed him a cab, and he collapsed inside.

After he'd given the driver his address, he relaxed back against the vinyl seat, his thoughts colliding together into one cohesive memory.

Running into Sophia before the meeting had startled him. Was it because he hadn't expected to see her? Or because he was simply tired.

He released a heavy sigh, eliciting a sideways glance from his driver.

Wade was no longer in love with Sophia—that, he knew. But he had loved her once, and a man does not forget a thing like that. Especially when, unlike other men, he did not find himself in love often.

Maybe, though, Wade had not been one-hundred-percent honest with himself regarding Sophia's wedding. He had been a bear that day, his thoughts dark and unyielding. He had since attributed his sour mood to the news he had received that very morning, news about EduCenter's sudden loss of funding.

But maybe more than that was in play that day. Perhaps his ego felt a little too much on display, his emotions so entangled in the past that they had become cinched in a knot. He hadn't needed to attend Sophia and Christian's wedding. Certainly, no one would have faulted him for skipping it altogether.

Wade glanced out the window, the passing lights a blur. In the end, he had wanted to be the better man that day. Not better than anyone in attendance, but the utmost best version of himself. To his folly, perhaps. His sister had often suggested, tongue-in-cheek she'd said, that his wealth was a result of more than his business acumen. She said he would rather deal with contracts and business propositions than matters of the heart.

Perhaps she had something there.

His mind drifted back to Priscilla. Not the beautiful woman he had seen tonight, but the one he met at the wedding. Her verve had attracted him, had even reminded him of himself when running with an idea that he was passionate about.

But she had thrown him off too. She was bold, penetrating, her unwavering gaze exposing him. The kind of thing that he would not allow—under any circumstances—when he was negotiating in business. Maybe he had sensed her crossing the line he had made where his heart was concerned and reacted by pushing back.

He pressed his forehead into his hand, trying to make sense of his thoughts. Had he been so guarded that he had nearly missed the opportunity that Priscilla now represented? He shook his head. She had offered him a pass tonight. When Sophia had come upon them and he had become disoriented, her smile had assured him.

Then why did a niggling in his gut cause him to question that assurance now?

The driver made a right turn down his street. As he pulled through the gated entry of his driveway, Wade unbuckled his seat belt, grabbed his bags, and headed into his home.

∼

EARLIER THIS EVENING, Priscilla had locked up the spa and slipped into the hallway of the inn, thankful for another day in the books. She'd had plans—big plans for the rest of the night. First, she would slip out of her heels, then she'd put on her silky loungewear, pour herself a glass of Chianti, and flop open the novel about the mountains of Tuscany that she'd been reading in fits and starts all week.

Instead, she dragged herself into her condo, listless. She tossed her keys into a tray by the door, plunked herself down onto the love seat, and began flicking through channels on her remote control. In the past hour, she had watched one-third of three different streaming shows, none able to keep her interest.

Priscilla inhaled and slowly let out a breath, the image of Wade's reaction to Sophia pulsating in her brain. She licked her top teeth and shut her eyes, trying to think about something—anything—else.

But her eyes opened again and she was back where she'd started.

Priscilla stood abruptly. She wandered into the kitchen, opened the fridge, and stared into it. Nothing suited her, but basic biology told her that too many hours without nourishment would not help her make better choices in the night ahead.

She grabbed a yogurt and slammed the fridge door shut.

On the couch again, she stirred her yogurt and took a bite. Was it peach? Or blood orange? She swallowed another bite, still undecided. One thing she wasn't confused about: Wade had seemed flustered. She supposed that running into one's ex for the first time since she had married the other guy might have something to do with that. But Priscilla had stood beside him and waited. Patiently.

What had she expected? For him to wrap his arms around her and tell Sophia that, sorry, but he was very busy?

Well. Sort of, she did.

Instead, he nearly left her mid-conversation without saying goodbye. By some miracle—and what seemed like an afterthought to her—he suddenly seemed to remember that she was standing behind him. She took another bite of yogurt, uncomfortable in her own head space. Something about this entire line of thought felt dangerously self-defeating.

She put the container of half-eaten yogurt on her coffee table and fluffed her hair with her fingers. Then she twisted her hair into a coil and pulled it around her left shoulder so she could lie down on the couch comfortably.

No matter what she did to try to forget the whole thing, it weighed on her mind like a hot compress. Leo had been like that, though she hadn't been as hyper aware of it at the time. Or maybe she had been in denial. He'd often become so absorbed in conversation with someone—especially when it revolved around sports—that he'd forget her presence. Once, he left a sports bar without her. She had been in a booth, sipping wine and reading a book.

Her cab ride home that night had cost more than her high-end glass of wine.

Abruptly, she sat up. Wade had called her on the way out of town last week, saying he wanted to take her to dinner. Had he even mentioned that tonight?

She let out a groan and stood. This was not like her. Not one bit like her! She walked into the kitchen and tossed the yogurt container into the garbage.

Priscilla had learned the hard way that a man's promise could be easily broken. Especially if he was discontented. Was Wade discontent with his life? Could he ever find happiness with a woman ... with her? A dark and desperate thought occurred to her. Even though Sophia had happily moved on, Wade could very well still be in love with her.

Did she want to date a man who might be carrying a torch for someone else?

She rolled over onto her back and stared at the ceiling. Priscilla had wanted to tell Wade about her thoughts on becoming a foster parent to Amber and to get his reaction. His advice, even. A prickle of a tear forced its way down her cheek and she let it ride. If they had spent any time together tonight, she would have told him and asked for his input—probably even his recommendation to the county too.

Priscilla bit her lip and gave her head a tight shake. She didn't want to overreact, like a high schooler might. But then again, had she not seen red flags more than once where Wade was concerned? She blew out a long, exhausted sigh. Then she closed her eyes and went to sleep.

~

She'd slept all night in her clothes from the day before, curled into a ball on the living room sofa. The effect this morning was not unlike a hangover—she felt unrested and annoyed with herself. Streaks of light warmed her upper arm, and she sat up, chagrined but not unforgiving.

Fuming last night had gotten her nowhere, evidenced by the shooting pain in her neck from sleeping on it wrong. When Leo had left her, she traveled through the stages of grief: denial, anger, and bargaining. But when she'd reached the fourth stage—depression—she said, "Enough!" and moved straight to acceptance.

The loss of her husband's love pained her more than she could ever explain. But if Leo no longer wanted to be married to her, nothing she could say or do would change that. She had learned, though, that she could have plenty of say in the care of her heart, her soul, and her mind.

So she'd laid it all out to God like a prayer. And he had

answered her in myriad ways. Why in the world would she think he'd stop now?

She stretched her limbs, drawing oxygen into her kinked muscles. In the minutes since she had awakened, the sun moved from slivers to wide beams of golden light. She had agreed to the evening shift at the spa, which meant her day was free for some self-care.

Quickly, Priscilla made herself some coffee, nibbled a bagel, and slipped into a swimsuit. Then she stepped out the front door, adventure buoying her mood.

A half hour later, her toes dug into the sand as she waited to rent a wetsuit and a SUP. She missed Amber, but they'd had so much fun that she couldn't think of a better way to spend her morning off.

As she waited for her board, she sent Amber a text:

PRISCILLA: *Had so much fun with you last week, that I'm renting a board again. Wish me luck!*

Amber: *Aw! Jelly! When're you coming out here again?*

PRISCILLA SIGHED. She hoped to drive out to the center soon. She had planned to talk to Wade about bigger needs that may be forming there but laid that thought aside. Besides, if her plans came to fruition, she and the teen would have many more opportunities to spend time together. Priscilla glanced out to sea, where flickers of light bobbed on the water. Guilt tugged at her heart. Should she have gone to the center today?

"Good to see you again!" Brett said. "No wahine with you?"

She smiled at the moniker the man had used for Amber, another tug on her heart at the absence of the girl. "Unfortunately, it's only me today. I'll bring her back sometime soon, though."

He nodded and flashed her a smile. "It's a good day, but be careful out there. Sun brings out the risk takers. Should be wide open, since it's morning, but keep a keen eye over your shoulder so you stay safe."

"Mahalo," she said, taking the paddle from him.

She watched as another newbie attempted to mount her board from the dock only to send up a shout and land with a splash in the murky channel water. No, thank you, she thought, and instead, headed for the man-made beach where she and Amber had launched from the previous week.

As she'd been taught, Priscilla waded into the water, careful not to scrape the fin of her board on the sandy floor of the sea. Once safely out, she launched herself onto the grip pad, knees first, and carefully stood. She held the paddle for balance, slowly lowering it into the water on her right side. She gave it a swish, then switched to the left, straightening out her direction.

Up ahead the last of the morning's thin cloud bank began to dissipate. She paddled forward, slowly, evenly, breathing in deeply with each stroke. Shoulders upright, back straight. A flying fish made an arc over the front tip of her board and she reacted with a squeal. Out in the water like this made her feel ... young. Free. Small, too. Not in a bad way, but in the scheme of life. The water stretched farther than she could fathom, and when she thought about that, she realized that her problems, aka her uncertainty regarding Wade, and love relationships in general, were a mere drop. Not unimportant—but not unsurmountable either.

She continued to paddle, the soft bounce of water creating a rhythm beneath her feet. Three large black cormorants stood on the dock to her left, wings outstretched. Pricilla had been teased mercilessly when she'd first come out here after reading CJ Capra's novel about a mermaid. She didn't care. Christian's whimsical fantasy had caught the eye of readers far and wide—including her. What she loved about it too, were the seagoing references. She'd learned some things while feasting on his best-selling novel, and she'd come away feeling smarter somehow.

She glanced again at those three stoic birds, their sleek black wings still widespread. She'd read that cormorant wings had less preen oil than other birds, so they absorbed water. Hence, the routine of drying out their wings in the sun.

If she were to try that, her arms would be weighed down by fatigue. She laughed and made a mental note to press some weights in the gym on her days off.

Priscilla continued to paddle out toward the harbor mouth, aware of her lack of a safety net. How could one moment hold both promise and panic? If she were to fall ... she dared not think about it.

But if she were to fall out here by herself? She would do what she always did—she'd force away the tears and pull herself out of the pit, salt water and all.

∽

PRISCILLA RETURNED HER RENTED SUP, showered off near the parking lot, and pulled a baby blue cover-up over her swimsuit. Remnants of salt and coconut oil still reached her senses. In her car again, she started it up, plugged in her phone, and opened the sunroof to allow fresh air to billow in. A flurry of texts pinged her phone and she snapped a peek at the screen, hoping nothing urgent messed with the blissful peace that had settled on her. The first one was from Wade:

WADE: *Good morning. Call me when you're up.*
 And …
 Trace: *There's a surprise for you at the inn. A big one. Coming in soon?*
 Trace: *p.s. Some serious testosterone in the lobby for you.*

PRISCILLA BIT BACK A SMILE, something her morning excursion had put back into her life. She would have to be careful where Wade was concerned, especially after allowing her heart to be exposed to him as freely as she had. But there was no harm in talking to him, in letting him say what he wanted to say to her. A night's sleep and morning on the water had brought her to that conclusion.

A light breeze entered through her open sunroof. See? When you refuse to wallow, life had a way of ironing itself out, didn't it? She glanced down at her cover-up, mulling whether it truly covered enough for her to stop in at the hotel lobby. She had a pair of capris and espadrilles in the car that she could change into, so she figured *why not?* and headed for the inn.

A catcall split the air as she hurried inside the lobby doors. Her red hair was still piled on top of her head and she reflexively touched the back of it with her fingers.

The minute she strolled inside, Trace waved her over. "You smell like coconut oil."

"I've been out at the beach. You said you had a surprise for me?"

Trace grabbed a flyer advertising nearby golf and fanned herself with it. "My goodness, Priscilla, you have a way of attracting some of the hottest oldsters in these parts."

Priscilla frowned. "Oldsters?"

"I don't mean that they're, you know, ready for the old folks home or anything like that. Not geezers," she said, laughing. "But first Mr. Prince gets all googly-eyed about you, and now some older gentleman from Virginia checks in, wanting to know where you are."

Her insides began a slow and uncomfortable descent like she was standing inside a hole-filled, sinking boat. She frowned. "How do you know he's from Virginia?"

Trace's finger flew across her computer keyboard. She turned the screen toward Priscilla. "Says so right there: Leonardo Shelby."

She took a step back, her pulse slowing more.

Trace pursed her lips. "One thing, though: He's got a little girl with him. She's cute. Maybe a grandchild?"

"Oh for goodness sake, Trace, he's in his forties." Priscilla frowned, took another step back, raising her palms. She wasn't surrendering—it was more like a "hands off" stance.

"Oh?" Trace said. "Well, then. You want his room number?"

She shook her head, her gaze darting for the inn's sliding doors. "No, I think I'll go home and maybe call in later ..."

"There he is!" Trace's face lit up with victory, as if pointing out a celebrity who had strolled out of a backstage door.

A trickle of sweat ran down Priscilla's neck and slipped beneath her cover-up. She set her chin and turned.

"Priscilla? It really is you." Leo approached her, eyes smiling, cheeks dimpled, as if they had not parted on less-than-amicable terms.

She wanted to run away. To dart for the nearest door and

never return. Instead, she slowed her breathing and jerked a look at her ex-husband. She had loved him once.

His eyes traveled across her face, as if searching for some kind of recognition, or at the very least, a positive reaction. He gave her that same old smile, the crooked one that had once struck her as quirky. Now, it made her skin itch.

"You look beautiful," he said.

His words sounded too shallow to sink in. Instinctively, she crossed her arms in front of her. How dare he bring his family here, of all places?

Priscilla slid a look toward the concierge desk where Trace watched with curiosity. She had nothing to say to him but also had no interest in making a scene, something that could live on in the memories of her co-workers long after Leo had gone.

Then, as if light suddenly flickered on, she noticed the girl in his arms. A child. And she was ... breathtaking. Smooth, full cheeks with patches of pink. Hair of blonde ringlets ... like her mother's.

Priscilla pulled her gaze away from the cherub. "What are you doing here?" she said to Leo, emotionless, which surprised her. She thought if she were ever to see her ex-husband again she'd shrug it off. *C'est la vie* and all that. But seeing him here tripped a wire inside her heart and she wanted to do something that simply was not her style—she wanted to scream.

Leo reached out and grazed her cheek with the backs of his fingers. She turned aside, like a flinch. But as she did, the child in his arms stirred.

Slowly, Priscilla raised her gaze from the stone tile that made up the inn's lobby and landed it on the little girl. She bit the inside of her bottom lip. The child peered at Priscilla, eyes watery blue like the sea. The moment froze. It wasn't this tiny child's fault that her parents had betrayed Priscilla in the way that they had.

The girl stretched her small body away from Leo. She reached precious pudgy hands to her, and on instinct, Priscilla scooped her up, rocking her as she held her close.

"Her name's Mia." Leo flexed his hands and popped his knuckles. "She's three. Brought her here by myself."

Mia pressed her cheek to Priscilla's chest and curled her arms in front of her small body, telegraphing her need.

"Are you tired?" Priscilla asked quietly.

Mia nodded, then stuck a thumb in her mouth. She didn't know much about three-year-olds, but she sensed this child needed some reassurance, as well as a woman's touch.

Priscilla looked up. She cleared her throat, her head full of questions. Yet she did not wish to startle the child. Mia had wedged her head between Priscilla's chin and upper chest, and she appeared to have fallen asleep.

"Let's sit in the lobby," Priscilla said, leading the way. She did not wait for Leo's reply, but lowered herself carefully onto a tufted leather sofa.

"You are still as strong as ever," he said, sitting next to her, his hands folded together. "Mia may look tiny, but when she's asleep, it's like dead weight in your arms."

He did not offer to take Mia from her. Priscilla adjusted herself, sliding a fat pillow beneath one of her elbows. The shock of seeing Leo—and his child—was beginning to fade. She met his gaze head-on. "I asked you what you were doing here."

His eyes creased at the corners. "I came to find you."

"Why?"

His voice deepened, the sound of it like an echo from their past. "I've missed you."

She narrowed her eyes, and a doubt-filled smile found its way to her face. "I don't believe you."

Leo shifted, putting one arm on the back of the couch behind her. He was facing her now on that sofa, an urgency in his gaze. He used to make a similar move when watching a game on TV or when reaching for the last slice of pizza. Rarely, though, when focused on her.

Leo raked a hand through his thinning hair. What he'd lost up top he had made up for in his scruffy beard, and, reluctantly, she admitted to herself what Trace had already alluded to earlier: Leo wore it well. He showed no signs of his back injury from years before, and today he looked tan and fit, as if he had become a member of an outdoor gym. A quick assessment reminded her why she had been drawn to him from the very start.

But that ended on close inspection.

Despite the abundance of laugh lines, his eyes were tinged with red. Fatigue appeared to weigh on him, his eyes smaller than she had remembered. And he popped his knuckles often. Nerves, maybe?

"You're going to make this hard on me, aren't you?"

"Depends on what 'this' is. You still haven't told me why you're here, Leo."

He scooted closer. "Call me darling. Like you used to."

She frowned and slowly wagged her head side to side. "If you missed me, you could have called." She paused. "I could have saved you the trip."

He hung his head yet his eyes flipped a look up at her, like a little boy who had been caught doing something naughty but who hoped for a reprieve anyway. "Let's start over."

"Absolutely. I'll begin. Where's Marnie?" Priscilla was unwilling to allow him to skirt the issue of the other woman.

"Gone."

"On a trip?" Priscilla had suspected this. Marnie had always liked her girls' weekends. Leo had likely begun to grow tired of her shenanigans and had decided to go on an adventure of his own. She could not allow herself to be dragged into something so ... tawdry.

His mouth turned down, a cheerlessness to it. Something akin to real emotion developed in his eyes, which pooled. "She's gone ... for good." His voice cracked.

Instinctively, Priscilla tightened her grip on the child. Tension crept across her forehead. "No. That can't be. Not without her child," she whispered.

He rolled a look at her, their eyes clashing. In his returned gaze, she saw that he was telling the truth. He swallowed and put a finger to his mouth, gesturing with a glance at his daughter.

Priscilla released a sigh and pressed her back into the sofa. Her extremities turned cold, a white-hot anger roiling through her. What he was telling her was unfathomable. How could a mother leave her child like this?

Mia pushed away from her, suddenly awake. The spot where she had laid her head swam with sweat. She rubbed her eyes with the back of her hands repeatedly. "We going to the beach?" Her voice sounded so tiny.

Priscilla sent a doubtful look at Leo. A sliver of a smile appeared on his face. "Well," he said, wicking a look over her, "you're dressed for it."

She twisted pursed lips at him, torn over how much anger she should allow to spill out. Concern niggled at her, though. He was as handsome as ever, but with frayed edges somehow.

Could his injury return? The one that had put him out of commission for enough time to fall out of love with her?

She shook off her thoughts, which were none of her concern anyway. That life was over and she had no interest in resurrecting it.

Instead, she gave Mia a quick smile. "Sure, honey. I'd be happy to show you the beach."

Ten minutes later they stepped onto the sand, Priscilla still wavering from the shock of Leo—and Mia's—sudden appearance. She crossed her arms in front of her as they walked, but stole another glance at him. When had she ever seen him in shorts and flip-flops?

"That's unusual attire for you," she said, making conversation.

"As they say, 'when in Rome'."

"Hmm. They do say that, yes."

He put Mia down and she ran on ahead of them, chasing after a band of sandpipers poking their beaks into packed, wet sand. "Shoo!" she said. "Shooooo!"

Leo laughed.

"What happened?" Priscilla asked, keeping her eyes on Mia, the roar of waves in their ears.

"She said it was too much. That she never wanted to be a mother."

Ridiculous. Priscilla could still hardly imagine this to be true. Who abandons their child? She blew a breath into the wind. "What are you going to do?"

"I don't reckon I know the answer to that right now." He slid a glance at her, holding her eyes longer than felt comfortable to her. "Had to get away from there—everybody hates me, you know."

She knew, but something else she had learned the hard

way: people weren't all that comfortable around her anymore either. Some from back home had either whispered when she walked by or flashed accusing glances at her, as if she'd had something to do with Leo's betrayal.

And those had been her friends.

Well, Leo had made his bed, so to speak. And he had chosen to stay in the town where they once lived together—in their old house—with a new woman and their child. He'd flipped the bird to those who had seen his sins up close and cemented himself right there in the midst of them.

She almost felt sorry for him. Almost. Raising a child alone was not for cowards—no matter what precipitated the situation. At least he hadn't shrunk away from his responsibilities.

Mia galloped along the beach, arms flailing. She suddenly stopped, put her hands onto her thighs, and stooped over.

Priscilla came alongside the little girl who was staring intently at the sand. She bent down. "What did you find?"

"Birdies," Mia said, pointing at air holes in the wet sand.

Priscilla scooped up some of the sand, and along with it came a crab on its crusty back, its antennae cycling in the air. "This is a sand crab."

"San cwab," Mia said. She poked it with her finger and squealed, the sound of it searing Priscilla's eardrum.

Priscilla released the creature back into the surf, then picked up a rough-surface clam shell and handed it to the little girl.

Mia laughed and pitched it onto the sand with a grunt. She picked up another shell and threw that into the air, too, watching it flip before landing on the soft sand. The remnant of a wave approached them, and Priscilla scooped up Mia before the cold water could reach her. Mia's giggles could be heard above the pound of the surf.

"You're a natural." He was close behind her, oblivious to the pain his observation caused. How many times had she told him how much she longed for this very thing?

When Priscilla set the little girl down again, safely clear of the roving surf, Mia bounded along, a permanent smile on her face. When she caught up to her again, Mia reached up and grasped her fingers. They walked along together until reaching a flat, wet congregation of small rocks. Priscilla crouched down and began to sift through the rocks, looking for sea glass that could very well be hidden beneath the layers like diamonds.

Mia joined her on the hunt, and beneath the shadows of her eyelashes, Priscilla gazed at the little girl. She swallowed the lump that had welled in her throat.

Why couldn't this have been her life?

CHAPTER 11

Wade had been sleeping for hours. Or was it days? He flicked a look at his phone, one eye open. He groaned and laid his head back down. Apparently, it only felt like days. The last time he had been sick had been years ago. So many that he could not exactly recall when that was, but one thing he knew: he had worked through it.

This time, though, whatever had knocked him out for the twenty-four hours had hit hard. He pulled himself into a seated position and stuffed a couple of pillows behind his back. Then he emptied his lungs with a long exhale.

Had Priscilla called him?

He looked at his phone and frowned, scrolling through the missed calls and voicemails. Nothing from her. No texts either.

His thumb hovered over her name on his phone, but the time caught his eye. He was late. Wade threw his phone onto the bed and pulled back the covers. After the raucous meeting at the inn the other night, he had promised to meet with Jackson and Sophia to discuss tweaks they might consider to the hotel as well as to the management of it. They had been planning to speak for some time, and now that Sophia was back, she said she was ready to pull her mind away from fashion for a little while and focus on what the inn needed from her.

Quickly, Wade showered and shaved. He felt ten times better than he had when he had fallen into bed the night before, but did he look it? He leaned closer to the mirror, peering into it. There were still visible remnants of bags beneath his eyes. He frowned and rubbed some lotion on his face that had been included with a purchase of his cologne. When had he ever spent quite so much energy *primping* for a meeting?

His phone rang and he grabbed it from his bed. "Good morning, Laura."

"Have you checked your email?"

She sounded testy—not what he needed now. "Why don't you tell me what it says."

"There's an issue with an inspection of the building in New York. Something about possible asbestos."

Wade screwed up his mouth. Of course there was asbestos—it was a pre-war building. He drew in a breath and blew it out with a rush. "Have the other parties responded?"

"Yes, all of them have with sarcasm-laced replies. You're the only one who has not added his two cents, but I knew you'd want to."

His mind began to race, as it usually did when a matter pressed in, especially something as lucrative as this one. As he considered his response, a vague image pushed aside his thoughts. The other evening came into view, the night he ran into Sophia in the hall of the inn. He thought a moment.

Where had they left things that evening? Did he even say goodnight to her?

Most of that evening was a blur, hence the plan for a more in-depth discussion today. Laura waited on the phone. Finally, he said, "I'll defer to the others."

"You're kidding."

"I am not. I have a meeting to attend. If you hear of anything urgent, send me a text. Otherwise, I will be out of reach for the next few hours."

By the time he arrived at the inn's cafe for his meeting with Jackson and Sophia, most of the breakfast crowd had gone. Not a bad thing when business was on the agenda. It appeared they would have much of the place to themselves. He glanced at his phone. He'd called Priscilla on the way over here, but he'd had to leave a voicemail.

Jenny approached him. "Will you be meeting anyone?"

He nodded. "There will be three of us."

She smiled and picked up several menus. "Right this way."

Jenny led him to a table toward the back of the restaurant, close enough to enjoy the view of the sea, but far enough away from the main hub that they could speak freely. The path along the water's edge was busier than usual when the fog made the resort less of a draw.

Still, he sensed someone familiar. Priscilla walking along that path at a fast clip. He watched her for a few seconds, mesmerized by the way she moved, by the confidence she imparted with each step. Even on her way to work in the spa, she dressed up. He wasn't much for noticing a woman's clothing style, but how could he miss the red heels, the belted, white dress that flared as she walked, and the oversized bag she held at the crook of her elbow?

He stood, put his napkin on his chair, and grinned at her

through the window. She stopped as if sensing him standing there, watching her. When she spotted him, she slowed. The expression on her face darkened, even as her ruby lips smiled.

When she changed course and entered the cafe, he stood up to greet her. She smiled up at him, though her expression of uncertainty unsettled him.

"Hi," he said.

"Hi." She tipped her head up, her eyes fully on him. He had craved that look from her.

Gently he brushed her cheek with a kiss. "You look more like you're about to stroll along the French Riviera rather than tame wild hair."

Her smile seemed forced. "Speaking of my hairstyling career, it's time for me to go." She glanced at his table before flickering her gaze back to him. "Are you meeting someone?

"Jackson and Sophia will be meeting me for breakfast. We have a few ends to tie up."

She pressed her lips together and nodded. "Well then, perhaps I will see you later."

His phone, which he had laid on the table, dinged.

She began to walk away, but he stopped her, placing a hand on her elbow. "Wait." He searched her face. Her eyes didn't meet his this time, not fully. They darted to his phone, to outside, to his eyes, and around again.

"I'd like to see you later."

She appeared to consider this. "And I would like to see you too. But I have a client waiting for me now." She pulled away again. "Call me later?"

Her answer needled him. She owed him nothing, of course. Though they had shared several heart-to-hearts and some brief kisses, he had not made steps toward a deeper commitment. Nor had she.

Yet he had hoped for the stars he had seen in her eyes so many times before today to be directed at him. He reached for her hand, but her fingers slipped away from him.

"Sorry we are tardy," Sophia said, approaching the table with Jackson close behind. "Hello, Priscilla," she called out over Wade's shoulder.

Priscilla waved hellos to both Jackson and Sophia, then continued to head to the exit that led to the salon and spa.

They ordered a late breakfast and began discussions about the corporate structure of Riley Holdings, which owned the inn and a couple of other smaller properties. As with many of his meetings with Jackson, the conversation strayed into memories of their father and how he would have wanted the company to run.

"I'm so glad you knew him," Sophia said, "and that you are able to help us understand how he would have wanted this business to continue."

Breakfast stretched into extra pours of coffee. When the cafe began to fill with guests at the lunch hour, they continued their meeting upstairs in Jackson's office.

"I should put you on retainer," Jackson quipped after Sophia noted the time.

She kissed her brother on the top of his head. "I have to go and make some beautiful clothing," she said. "I'm sure you and Wade can continue this discussion without me."

She was right. He and Wade talked awhile longer—some about the business but even more so about baseball.

By the time he walked out of Jackson's office, relief poured through him. The infatuation he had once felt for Sophia had disappeared completely. She was lovely, as always, but even when she sat feet from him, he could not keep his mind off of Priscilla.

Wade determined to sweep Priscilla off those beautiful heel-clad feet of hers, so he strolled down the long, art-filled corridor to the salon.

"Hello, Katrina." He entered the glass-encased area. "Is Priscilla in?"

"Good afternoon," she said. "I'm sorry to say that you missed her. Short shift for her today."

He thanked her and left the salon, intent on Plan B: Call Priscilla and make plans to see her tonight. But Jackson intercepted him, stopping him with a pointer finger in the air. "Completely forgot to bring up a report that our risk manager sent us last week."

He frowned. Wade wanted to stay on target but had a soft spot for the inn. "Was the report negative?"

"Depends on who you ask."

Wade smiled ruefully at that. "Send it on to my office and I'll give you my opinion."

"He did mention that there are some issues with the pool. I realize that's not necessarily your area of expertise, but I'd like to point to a few things as I walk you out." He stopped. "Can you take a walk with me?"

"Of course."

The designated pool and spa area teemed with visitors today, and he questioned the decision to wear one of his dark suits outside among the revelers. The sun had heated the day to an extent that even his worsted wool suit, lightweight as it was, would soon turn uncomfortably warm. He and Jackson found a place to stand toward the back of the pool's deep end, where palm and banana trees created a lush backdrop for those wishing to steer clear of rowdy children and the spray of errant cannonballs.

Jackson squinted, his gaze toward the shallow end of the

pool where the sun shone brightest. "Is that Priscilla over there?"

Wade took a step forward and noticed her there too, by the edge of the pool. She was kneeling on one of the inn's large striped pool towels, the skirt of her sundress splayed around her. A small girl with white-blonde hair sat on the pool steps, splashing and laughing as Priscilla cooed at her.

It reminded him of the way Priscilla took to Sadie when he'd brought her to Meg and Jackson's party.

He turned to Jackson. "Excuse me for a moment."

She didn't notice him approaching her, at least, not at first. When she did, she seemed to startle, her eyes blinking rapidly, perhaps from the brightness of the sun.

That's when he noticed the man in the pool who protected the child from wandering off of the steps. He seemed to close in on both the girl and Priscilla as she looked up to acknowledge Wade.

"You're here," she said, raising her hand toward him. He took it, helping her to stand, which she did in her bare feet. Her smile was warm, but a question lingered in her eyes, too.

He felt a question forming as well. "I stopped by the salon," he said, "but Katrina said you had already gone."

She slid strands of hair behind her ear. "I came in for a couple of locals who requested me today. I'm already finished for the day."

A child's voice came between them. "Pa-silla! Pa-silla!"

Priscilla squatted back down and stroked the child's head. "Yes, love?"

The barrel-chested man in the water spoke up. "Look at that. She sure has taken to you like nobody I've ever seen."

Priscilla turned away from the girl, peering up at Wade over her shoulder. "Wade, this is my former husband, Leo.

And this"—she said, gesturing to the girl on the steps—"is Mia. His daughter."

The guy in the water was her ... ex?

Leo cracked a smile and flicked his chin toward Jackson. "Saw you and your friend over there lookin' like a couple of guys from *Men in Black*."

Wade stuck a hand in his pocket. He said hello and briefly nodded at Leo before sending a questioning look at Priscilla. When she didn't add any insight to the situation, he began to back away. "I'll leave the three of you to enjoy your day."

"Wade—wait." Priscilla followed him but he had to think. He kept walking through the gated exit and into the inn's parking lot until she took ahold of his elbow. "Why are you acting like this?"

He turned around, his jaw aching from the way he had been clenching it. "What way am I acting?"

She let go of him and crossed her arms in front of her middle. "Like you're upset with me." She paused. "If anyone should be upset, it's me."

"None of this makes sense, Priscilla. After all you've said about that guy"—he spiked a thumb toward the pool area—"and now you're frolicking at the pool with him. And his child?"

"How do you know his wife isn't here with him?"

He swept a gaze across her face, searching. Had she forgiven them both for their betrayal? Guilt washed over him. Priscilla would forgive; he knew that about her. But had she forgotten? Already?

She shook her head, her expression displaying her conflicting thoughts. "I'm sorry. That wasn't fair." She let out a sigh. "His wife isn't here."

Wade furrowed his brow. "Are you saying he came here to see you?"

She pressed her lips into a line and nodded, that same unsure look in her eyes.

He shifted, unable to take his eyes off of her. "What did you mean that you should be angry with me? What do I have to do with any of this?"

She reached up and fiddled with his tie, her face a mask. All of a sudden, she put on a smile and looked him in the eyes. "It was nothing. Really."

He reached down and stilled her hand, folding it in his. "Then why did you say it?"

She gave one of her shoulders a little shrug and kept smiling, though it wasn't the light-up-your-face kind of expression he had gotten used to seeing on her. "Forget what I said. If I've learned one thing, it is not to focus on the negative things that life serves up."

Wade cocked his head to one side. "And that's why you invited Leo and his young daughter here? To let go of your negative thoughts of them?" He sighed and let her hand go. "I find that difficult to understand, Priscilla."

"I did not invite them here. Leo decided to come on his own accord, and no matter what he has done to me in the past, I cannot fault his daughter."

He took a step back and crossed his arms, his warm-weather suit suddenly suffocating. "Looks like you can't ignore her either."

Something in her eyes flashed. "Is that required?"

He unhooked his arms and turned his palms out. "I've got a meeting and I'm already late."

Priscilla stared at him, her tentative smile gone, replaced by a grim stare.

Wade slid into the driver's seat of his car and slammed the door shut. He let out a heavy breath and glanced back to see Priscilla turn and walk back toward the inn's pool.

He had been in a similar place before—first with Rose and later with Sophia, but this time, he had not allowed himself to fall headlong into anything that would cause him immeasurable heartbreak. Not again. As he drove out of the inn's parking lot, Wade decided to protect his heart at all costs.

He just hoped it was not too late.

∼

When Priscilla returned to the pool, Mia was out of the water and sitting on a lounge chair, licking a juice bar from the poolside food service. Her hair was a matted mess, but she was safe and wrapped in a towel.

"Hi, Pa-silla," Mia said.

Priscilla scooted in next to her. "Hello, sweetie. Is that a good popsicle?"

Mia nodded her head vigorously, causing the red juice from the popsicle to smear up and down her face.

"That guy someone you're into now?" Leo asked. "Didn't seem like your type."

Priscilla began to smooth Mia's wet hair with her fingers. "You know, I have some yummy-smelling lotion that I could put into your hair so it won't tangle." She leaned closer to Mia's ear. "Would you like me to put some on your hair?"

Mia nodded again, possibly oblivious to what Priscilla meant, but enthusiastic just the same. Priscilla stood up and looked at Leo. "I'm going to run over to the salon and get some detangler for her. It will make her life much easier."

He flashed her a smile. "And mine."

"Mm-hm, yes."

"You're not going to tell me about the guy?"

"He's none of your business. Now, wait here. I'll be right back with some product."

Priscilla dashed off to the salon, her mind heavy with unshed emotion. She didn't know whether to cry or pitch a fit, but she wanted to do one of those things. At least one. Negativity stuck to her like hot sweat, her body feeling like she had just walked through New York City on a muggy summer day.

Liddy approached her, concern lining her face. "Hi, Priscilla. You doing okay?"

"Yes, of course." She flashed a smile. "I was lost in thought, that's all."

Liddy hugged her clipboard to her. "I'm relieved to hear that. Otherwise, I was going to ask you next whose butts I should kick for you."

Priscilla let out a shocked little laugh. "Excuse me?"

"Ha—I'm kidding." Her forehead bunched and she reached out and touched Priscilla's upper arm. "I hope you know how much we all love you around here. Meg's been so happy that you moved so close, and customers adore your work. You're such a blessing, girl."

Priscilla began to blink, the torrent about to burst. "Thank you so much, Liddy. I-I don't know what to say to that other than, I am grateful. For all of you." Her voice cracked and she reached for the salon door, thankful to have a reason to turn away from Liddy's precious presence.

Once inside, she darted for the supply room, thankful that Katrina and the others were too busy at the washbowls and behind dryers to pay attention to her. Inside the fully stocked room, Priscilla wavered. She reached for one of the shelves and held on. *I will not cry, I will not ... cry!* "Lord," she whispered, "I'm so confused. Help me stay strong."

The supply room door swung open. "Oh my gosh," Katrina said. "You scared me to death! I thought you left a long time ago."

Priscilla forced a smile. "I only got as far as the pool. My friend's little girl needs some detangler and I was"—she turned, pretending as if she had been searching for just the right product all along—"looking for some in here."

Katrina tossed thick strands of black hair over one shoulder and reached up to a top shelf. Her bangles jingled in Priscilla's ear. "I like this stuff." She handed a spray bottle to Priscilla. "Gets all that chlorine out too."

"Ah, perfect. Thank you."

Katrina leaned her head to the side. "You sure you're okay?"

"Yes. I'm perfect." She held up the bottle and slipped past Katrina toward the exit. "Thanks again!"

By the time she reached the pool, Leo was resting on the lounger with Mia on his lap. The little girl's eyelids looked heavy, as if she were about to fade into a deep sleep.

Priscilla slowed to a stop in front of them. "I brought Mia some detangler." She held the bottle out for Leo to see. "But I guess now is not the best time."

At the sound of Priscilla's voice, Mia rousted. She rubbed her eyes. "You back, Pa-silla?"

She reached chubby arms toward her and Priscilla scooped her up. She found an upright patio chair and lowered herself into it, propping Mia on her lap. The little girl yawned. "Wus that?" she asked.

Priscilla showed her the white bottle with lively blue writing on it. "This is something that will make your hair not hurt when we brush it. May I spray some of it on your hair?"

Mia nodded forcefully, her expression stern. This was serious business, apparently.

After she sprayed on some of the product, Priscilla gently released the tangles in Mia's hair with her fingers. The little girl hummed softly during the entire process. What could have been a light moment turned dark in Priscilla's heart. The innocence of this child would someday be shattered by her mother's abandonment, and as she thought about that, she struggled to keep her emotions in check.

Mia yawned, her eyelids heavier now. She collapsed against Priscilla's chest, no longer able to keep those sweet eyes of hers open.

Priscilla looked up at Leo, who hovered nearby. "She's asleep, I think. Want to take her?"

He nodded and bent down to hoist the sleeping child into his arms. As he did, he stopped, his eyes inches from Priscilla's. "I've missed you so," he said.

She returned his gaze, but it was as if she were looking into the eyes of a stranger. She felt nothing more for him than what she might have for an old friend.

Priscilla turned away, separating herself from the situation, though Mia's predicament was making it more and more painful for her to do so. She smoothed imaginary wrinkles from her skirt and slipped errant strands of her red hair behind her ear.

"Priscilla?"

She raised her chin and crossed her arms, looking directly at Leo. Mia slept like an angel on his shoulder. "Yes?"

"I would like to see you again."

She dropped her gaze to the ground, tears welling. Then

she shook her head and looked at him dead on. "You look good, Leo."

He smiled, a sort of relief flooding his features.

She continued. "And you need to keep taking care of yourself, for your daughter's sake. I don't envy you ... nor her. If you don't take care of yourself, who will watch over Mia?"

"Mia already adores you." His eyes steadied himself on her, and she recognized that look. He would do that on those occasions when she shared her innermost thoughts with him and hoped he would join her—or at least dream with her. It was his defense mechanism—one that he used to manipulate her to his way of thinking.

Her heart sank lower than it had already fallen today because, she knew, she could not allow herself to fall for his tactics. Not ever again.

He continued, reaching out and touching her cheek with his rough hand. "How about we raise her together. You would like that, Priscilla. Wouldn't you?"

She forced herself not to look at the waif of a child draped over his shoulder. Instead, she met Leo's gaze with a hard stare of her own. "That's simply impossible, darling. Because you don't deserve me—and I'm in love with somebody else."

CHAPTER 12

The realization of Priscilla's feelings for Wade struck her mightily with one blow—one of those dawnings that could either empower or disable a person. Until recently, he had shown little interest in her beyond friendship. Could she believe that his attention to her had blossomed into something more substantial? Something sustainable?

And even if it did, how would he react to her intentions regarding Amber?

Priscilla hurried along the path to the beach, glancing at her phone. She could call him and tell him how she felt and see how he responded. That's what reasonable people did. It was also what people who lived their lives with no worries or fear did.

Her joie de vivre, however, had taken a direct hit lately, causing confusion to reign. Priscilla stuffed her phone into the pocket of her hoodie and gave herself the freedom to walk the beach without making any decision at all.

The sand felt spongy beneath her bare feet and she

reveled in the lick of cool water that pooled beneath them with each landing of a wave. Her phone rang, causing a ripple to travel through her chest. It was Amber.

"Hi, Cilla."

"Hi, yourself. What have you been doing today?"

"Nothin. Are you working?"

Priscilla's heart constricted. She'd promised Candace she would not let Amber know of her plans, not until she could be assured that she would succeed. The teen had been through enough disappointments. *As have I ...*

"I worked this morning already." She kept the afternoon's drama to herself. "I'm actually walking on the beach right now. It's a nice way to wind down."

"Lucky."

Priscilla drew in a breath of that fresh air. "The fog blew in again. Not wild about that, but I agree, I'm a blessed girl just being here. Hopefully, you'll be able to come and visit me soon."

Amber was quiet.

"Are you still there?"

"Yeah. I guess I'll go now."

"I'm happy to talk to you as I walk. Sure there's nothing else you'd like to talk about?"

"Not really. Well, maybe you could give me a haircut sometime. I mean, I don't have any money, but you could practice on me."

Priscilla laughed lightly. "I would adore that."

"Don't get too excited about it. I don't want it to be, you know, like super short or anything."

"Oh really? Shoot. I was thinking of chopping off enough to make a wig for my mannequin."

Amber laughed. "Cilla, you're so crazy! Oh, man, you got Wade so good that day."

Priscilla laughed back, the memory fast becoming a favorite. "Okay, I promise to give you a trim exactly the way you want it. We'll plan something soon. Okay?"

"'kay."

The call with Amber had given Priscilla the lift she needed, even if the fog in the sky refused to blow away. She glanced at the phone in her hand and dialed. The line rang so long she wondered if Wade would ever pick up.

~

WADE'S PHONE rang for the second time that evening. He scowled. How much more bad news did he care to hear? He glanced at the screen and saw that it was Priscilla. He puffed out a sigh and considered allowing her call to go to voicemail —but only briefly.

"Hi, Priscilla."

"Hello."

A thought pressed on him as the silkiness of her voice rolled over him: He wanted to tell her about the new hitch in his building sale, this one worse than the asbestos worry. Somehow, he knew she would have a way of making the predicament sound less daunting.

But he pushed that thought away. Too dangerous. Had he already forgotten the scene he had walked in on earlier today? She looked nearly angelic there at the edge of the pool, her white dress fanned about her, the tiny child gazing up at her. If he had not known better, he would have taken her for the girl's mother. The scene stung and he was having a difficult time pushing past it.

Priscilla interrupted his tangled thoughts. "I think we should finish our conversation from earlier, don't you?"

"Listen," he said, "something has come up regarding the deal I was working on in New York."

"You're unavailable. I understand."

"I didn't say that." The line went quiet, but he felt her there. Everything about this felt uncomfortable, like a rope against his skin. He swallowed. "It looks like I have to fly back to the City in the morning, but maybe it would be a good idea to meet for a drink. I'll pick you up in twenty minutes."

She did not answer right away, as if mulling her response. "No, that's not necessary at all. I'll meet you."

He nodded, sensing this might be for the best. "Fine. Let's meet at the seafood restaurant at the harbor."

"I know the place."

He hung up and left his home, noting how the fog in the sky created shadows.

∽

PRISCILLA CHANGED out of her dress and heels and slipped into capris, a cotton top, and espadrilles. She felt free and comfortable as she took the steps up to the restaurant, determined to pour out her heart to Wade about Leo and Amber ... and everything.

She'd had the rest of the afternoon and evening to think about the bizarre last couple of days. Saying goodbye to Leo for the second time had been easy. Saying goodbye to Mia? Getting over that would take some time.

The hostess asked if she was dining alone.

"No, there will be two of us."

The young woman counted out two menus. "Right this

way." She led Priscilla to a table at the far corner of the restaurant. After ordering a drink, Priscilla sat back and looked outside. Dozens of boats huddled together under a darkening sky. If she were a painter, she'd book this spot nightly until she'd captured the serenity of that view.

"Sorry I'm late," Wade said. He pecked her on the cheek and slid into the booth across from her. It was as if they hadn't had terse words at all earlier today in the parking lot of the inn.

"I ordered myself a glass of wine already," she told him.

He signaled for the waiter. "Whiskey. On the rocks." He turned to her, his face unreadable.

Then again, maybe this would not be as simple as she had hoped.

They sat in an unusual silence until their drinks were served.

"Cheers," she said, lifting her glass of Pinot Grigio.

"Salud." He clinked his glass with hers.

They each took sips, the quiet growing into an uncomfortable silence.

Wade clasped his hands around his drink. "I guess you feel we have some unfinished business."

She took that as her cue and reached forward, placing her hand on one of his. He stiffened, but she pressed on. "I wanted to explain that I had no idea that Leo had come to the inn until, well, until it happened."

He eyed her. "You weren't unhappy about it, I take it."

She mulled that. "I don't know if 'unhappy' is the right word, exactly. I was confused by it. Curious, even."

"Because you're not over him?"

She pulled back, frowning. "I am completely over him, Wade. But he took me by surprise."

Wade sat back too, flashing his palms up quickly, as if in surrender. "I'm not trying to be hard on you. Nor am I trying to sound like a jealous man."

"And I'm not accusing you of any of that."

"It is obvious to me, though, that you still have feelings for your husband."

"Former husband."

"Yes, right. You don't appear to be fully over him."

"I'm not ... over him?" Her voice sounded so small to her own ears.

His shoulders lowered, as if in defeat. But this time, he looked sad, rather than angry. "Look, I've been in this place—shoot, you know I have."

"What are you talking about?"

"Obviously, Sophia had feelings for someone else that I knew nothing about. And you told me you witnessed her dump me after I proposed."

She scoffed and pulled back. "I didn't exactly say that."

"It's what you meant."

She reached across the table again, but he pulled his hand back. At that, she put her hands into her lap, folding them together, a knot forming at the base of her throat.

Wade's voice turned softer, earnest. "You are an incredible woman, Priscilla. But in my gut, I sense that you are not ready for a relationship."

She kept her gaze down. How dare he? He was wrong, far beyond wrong. But would it matter if she corrected him? By the tone of his voice and the line drive of his gaze, he had made up his mind. *C'est la vie*, right? Isn't that how she had lived her life, especially since Leo left? Letting go had become as much a part of her as living.

She turned a calm, expressionless look on him. "If that's what you think."

His mouth dropped open, those dark eyes of his shrouded by brows that lowered, crinkling his forehead. "That's it?"

She took another sip of her wine, set the glass down, and offered him a smile. "Darling, if that's what you think, there is nothing I can do to change your mind."

His quirked his mouth. "So everything is fine. Whatever I say is fine. Whatever I think is fine?"

She pressed her lips together, her own brows rising in agreement. "What else do you want from me?"

His sharp gaze zeroed in on her, and he inhaled as if preparing himself for battle. "I don't know," he finally said. He folded his arms onto the table in front of him, settling himself onto them. "Maybe I want to see you fight a little. To get up in my face and tell me to mind my own business."

"But you have made up your mind. That is clear."

He set his jaw. She couldn't fathom why he would be angry at *her*. Hadn't she already told him that Leo meant nothing to her?

"Remember when we met out on the lawn?"

"Well, we had actually seen each other before that ..."

"Fine. Then do you remember when we talked outside of the chapel? Before Sophia's wedding? I want to know what happened to that woman."

She stared at him, hot anger rising in her as fast as she worked to stuff it down. She locked it away. She had no plans to unveil her inner thoughts to Wade, not the way he was acting now. What if she were to tell him how she felt and he trampled all over her feelings?

Pricilla had been there before. She flicked away the memory, but it circled back, like a bee to spilled vinegar. She had always maintained that she'd let Leo walk away with nary a protest. But that had not been completely true. When she had first learned what Leo had done—what he and Marnie had inflicted upon their marriage—she'd told him right then and there, "I forgive you and I'll take you back." Perhaps she never liked to recall that moment because she had felt so desperate at the time.

But Priscilla had made a vow to Leo—for better or for worse. His infidelity had been worse than she had ever envisioned could happen to them. Even so, she had responded in the way that she thought she should.

And Leo had walked away from their marriage anyway. Scratch that, he had asked her to leave so that he and Marnie could live in *their* house.

She looked at Wade as he sat across from her, handsome and troubled. Maybe he would not throw away her feelings as carelessly as an ex-husband, but she did not want to give him that chance.

Wade furrowed his brow again. He licked his lips, ignoring his whiskey. "When I met you, I was taken aback. You were so ... so bossy."

She leaned her head to the side, examining him. "Bossy?"

"You got under my skin, no matter how I tried to fight it."

"So you were trying to fight me?"

"Maybe fight wasn't the best word choice." He sat back and swiped his hand through his thick head of salt-and-pepper hair. "I like you, Priscilla. But this thing with Leo ... I don't know what to think about that."

She sensed an old wall rising within her. That wall had helped her when she had graduated from beauty school. Making conversation had never come that easy for her, but she had practiced listening well and had made an art of it. Her clients back home could say anything they wanted to her—and had they ever. None of them, unless a very close friend, knew much about her at all.

And that same wall had made it possible for her to fly off to Europe by herself, making friends along the way as she had with Meg and others. Listening well, plus offering only the highlights of her own life, equaled safe living.

"I like you, too, Wade." Priscilla was careful not to divulge the extent of her feelings for him. She considered bringing up how she felt the other night when he'd left her alone to attend a meeting with Sophia, how his slight had affected her, but in the end, she knew she would sound ridiculous, desperate maybe. She continued, "But you don't believe me and I'm not sure that's something *I* can overcome."

She kept her voice calm, unwilling to let a man—any man—hurt her again. Either he was one hundred percent in or he was not at all. She had learned the hard way how easy it was for a committed man to break his promise. She couldn't be a victim again—she just wouldn't.

"Tonight wasn't what I thought it would be," she said simply. She considered picking up her purse and walking out.

"Me either."

She stared back at him. "What was it that you expected, Wade?"

He scowled, something she was beginning to grow tired of. She had seen a similar expression on his face when avoiding a call or when things did not appear to be going his way. It made her wonder if something more was happening with him, with his business, and if he would be as honest with her as he wanted her to be with him.

He interrupted her thoughts to answer her question. "I didn't expect the Pollyanna worldview. I thought—I thought we'd have a meeting of the minds, so to speak. That we'd fight it out."

"So you thought I asked you to a business meeting?" She shook her head. "Let me ask you: Why is it that you rely on money rather than your friends?"

"What are you talking about?"

"I've seen it firsthand, with the center. You would rather throw money at a situation rather than do the work to let others know of your troubles—as if life is some big business deal to you."

His eyes bored into hers. "So you do have some fight left in you."

She tried, but Priscilla couldn't muster a smile. Even at Wade's attempt at a joke.

"There."

"What?"

"You tried to smile, like we're not embroiled in a disagreement right now."

"It's called diffusing a difficult situation."

"Why diffuse it? Why not hit it head on?"

"Okay. Then answer my question about EduCenter." Her pulse raced. "My understanding is that you were behind the rise of Sophia's fashion design business—"

"Sophia's designs got her where she is today—not me."

"But you helped her with marketing, with social media. Correct?"

He shrugged. "That's something I've always dabbled in. It's not the main focus of my consulting business."

"Regardless, why not do the same for the center? Get more people involved? Your friends didn't even know the center existed."

His jaw clicked and she wanted to reach up and run her fingers over his skin.

"The center was doing fine before you became involved," he said.

She bit back a gasp, mentally withdrawing her hand from his face, the sting of his rebuke weighing on her. "In other words, you don't want me around."

He recoiled, his expression confused. "That's not what I said."

"You didn't have to." Priscilla took hold of her purse and slid out of her chair.

"I just meant that we had it under control."

She gave him a sad little smile. "You may think you can control everything, Wade, but you can't. Things happen. Like Leo showing up here—that was completely out of my control. The center has taken a financial hit. And your New York deal may not happen the way you want it to. Take your pick." Priscilla sighed. "If we don't learn to let go of what we think we can control, to understand God's hand in every situation, then we're in danger of being tossed around hopelessly."

The space between his eyes constricted. "Cilla ..."

Priscilla shook her head and slung her bag over her shoulder. She had so much more to say to Wade, about Amber, about how deeply she felt herself falling for him, but in the end, she had no fight left.

CHAPTER 13

Priscilla pulled up to the condo she was renting near the beach. Although she technically lived in the same complex as Jackson and Meg, the buildings were spread far and wide, with long, curled pathways lined with jacaranda trees with purple showy flowers and aromatic eucalyptus trees between them. They lived far enough away from each other to make it seem like they weren't neighbors at all.

There were other differences as well. While Jackson and Meg owned a large end unit with views of the sea and easy access to the pool, Priscilla's place was a small one-bedroom on the first floor. She had a tiny nest egg from her settlement with Leo, but she preferred not to touch that other than what she had put down as a deposit on this small rental. Instead, she survived on her salon salary, thankful for the generous tips from the inn's clientele.

Her one requirement when searching for a place was that she could hear the waves crashing at night. Check. Requirement number two? She wanted to be able to easily walk to the beach. With Meg's recommendation, she snagged her lovely condo.

She slipped out of her sandals, allowing her feet to burrow into thick long-pile carpet, and padded across her living room. Drinks with Wade had not gone well, obviously. Neither had her goodbye to Leo. It took mere minutes to fall in love with his child, to become swept up in what might have been. If she had told any of her friends back home, or her new ones here, they'd think she had lost her mind for even entertaining the thought of helping Leo raise his child.

It had nothing to do with him. Not really. Despite his betrayal, Mia's situation immediately drew her in—oh, and the way she looked at her? Priscilla shook her head and put a fist gently to her chest, holding back tears. She ached for Mia and promised herself to pray for Leo. He was going to need it.

Her mind wouldn't quiet. She'd tried to put on her most positive face with Wade, but he'd rebuffed her. Acted like she was weak. What did he want from her? Her mind drifted back to when she first encountered Wade before Sophia's wedding. Even then she recognized a red flag in his demeanor. He'd scowled at her, though she had given him a pass, assuming his bad mood had something to do with the fact that his ex-girlfriend was about to be married.

She'd seen his softer side, though, and she'd warmed to him. More than warmed—she heated up on the spot whenever he was near. The realization of that sent her into the throes of deep, wandering thoughts. Priscilla wanted him in her life—every part of it—this, she knew. But ... something held her back.

Perhaps it was knowing that Wade Prince was a little bit too good to be true.

She groaned and shook her head. Then she pulled on a

tufted coat and meandered along the lighted path that led to the beach, letting herself out through an iron gate. Her feet landed in soft sand, causing the tension to begin to flow out of her shoulders. A swirl of a breeze played with loose strands of her hair and she breathed it in, salt and all.

Priscilla began to trudge through sand toward the sea. The farther she moved from lighted buildings, the more she was ushered under a canopy of dark night lit by a haze of stars. She paused and tilted her gaze upward. Though not overly bright, the expanse of dark, star-punctuated night made her feel tiny as she stood beneath it. Like one of God's uncountable forever family members. And bonus: the tinier she felt, the more her worries shrank.

She closed her eyes, allowing the sound of the sea to center her, the scent of ocean spray to wash away her worries. She swung a look northward, and if she were to squint real hard, she could see the tip of Sea Glass Inn staring back at her, a stalwart on a precipice by the sea. A sense of thankfulness for her new second home fluttered through her.

She turned around at the sound of a familiar laugh flowing in on the breeze. A couple approached, light from their phones leading the way.

"Meg," Priscilla said, as they approached.

"Hey there!" Meg shined her light at her and laughed again. "Sorry about that. Yes, it's us. What're you doing out here tonight?"

Jackson cut in. "Same thing as us. Obviously."

Priscilla looked closer. "Is that Jax you're wearing?"

Meg laughed. "Best babysitter ever." She patted Jaxson's bum through the baby papoose that hung over her shoulders. "Cheap and he falls asleep every time."

A familiar pang of desire tugged at her, made more

pronounced by the events of the past two days. But she painted on a smile. "Looks like a perfect setup."

"Beautiful night," Jackson said.

She gave the sky an obligatory sweeping glance before returning her gaze to the lovebirds. "It is. I couldn't resist coming out here. It's cool, but not cold, you know?"

"Oh but that breeze." Instinctively, it seemed, Meg pulled the blanket draped over her shoulders more tightly around herself and Jax.

Priscilla sensed their conversation dying. "Well," she said, "you two enjoy your night. I'll see you at the inn."

Meg reached out and touched her upper arm. "Yes, we will."

"Or maybe at the pool," Jackson said.

Priscilla smiled and waved as she walked away, realizing something. For the first time since she had moved across the country, she had begun to feel her singleness. Despite the problems she and Leo had in their marriage, they had been a couple. For those years, she always had another person to go home to at the end of the day, for better or worse. Worse, mostly.

Maybe knowing that something appeared to be happening between her and Wade had raised her hopes. And now that things with him had sputtered so spectacularly, she had gained a heightened awareness of what she had lost. Even though it never actually existed.

Her cell phone in her pocket rang, and she jumped at the sound of it. Amber's number. "Hello?"

"Hey." The teen's simple greeting, delivered in that voice she had come to love, was a balm to her soul. Especially right now.

"Hey, yourself. What are you up to tonight?"

"Nothin'."

Priscilla could almost hear the shrug in Amber's voice. She was bored and decided to call her—all she needed to know.

"I was thinking you should come out here again on Thursday. Mari wants a donut bun in her hair."

"Of course. Like a ballerina bun. I think we could do that."

"I don't want one. Lame."

"Why not? I thought you liked the waterfall braid I gave you once."

"Yeah, that was cool, but not the same as a bun in my hair."

"It would show off those gorgeous high cheekbones of yours."

"Yeah, okay. Save that for the girly girls." She paused and Priscilla could hear gum snapping. "I was thinking we could go to the beach or something."

Priscilla laughed, the first real one in days. Amber often seemed to skip from thought to thought.

Amber continued. "Hey, so, some of us were wondering if you, you know, were thinking of dating Wade."

Case in point.

Priscilla paused, her mind searching for anything she might have said about Wade to the girls. "Why would they wonder that?"

Amber was quiet. Priscilla pictured that shrug again. Maybe a scowl too. "I don't know," Amber finally said. "Staci said she was watching you for a super long time last time you guys were here."

"Hm. Well, tell her thank you for watching out for me, but I don't see that happening."

"How come?"

Maybe it was the crystal night air or the stirring up of oxygen in her blood, but for whatever reason, a moment of transparency came over her. "Wade isn't interested in me, Amber. At least, not in that way."

"So he told you that to your face? Rude."

A smile burgeoned, though it was short-lived. "Darling, this is one of those complicated adult things that you will have to learn about soon enough. Don't trouble yourself another minute. Promise?"

"I guess."

"Now, about that ballerina bun, I'll have a look at my schedule, but I think Thursday could work. Will you girls be there then?"

"Yeah. Nothing else to do around this town."

"Your town's loss is my gain!"

"Huh?"

Priscilla laughed lightly, thankful for levity. A cool breeze stirred, she said goodnight to Amber, and hung up.

Haze rolled across the sky, leaving the stars to fight for air. Priscilla crossed her arms and tucked her hands into her sleeves to keep them warm. The beach was empty. Her mind was not. If the sun had not set and taken all its heat with it, she could have walked deep into the night. Instead, she made her way back home, her quads and calves complaining with each step through deep sand.

∾

Once she reached her complex, Priscilla unlocked the gate and began down the path to her condo. She had almost reached her front door when a scrape against the concrete caught her attention. She looked up. Meg?

"Hey," Meg said.

"What are you doing here? I mean ... is everything all right?"

Meg watched her curiously through the light of a nearby lamppost. "That's what I came to find out."

"Oh. I'm confused. What about your family?"

"They are completely fine. Jackson was tired, so he put Jax to bed and he'll probably watch TV until he falls asleep."

Priscilla wasn't sure what all of that meant. Did Meg want to talk to her about something? Or was she out here, wandering around because family life was harder than it looked?

"Priscilla," Meg broached, "you seemed melancholy out there tonight." She swung her gaze toward the west briefly. "Want to talk about it?"

Priscilla put a smile on her face. She shook her head. "Is that what's on your mind tonight? I'm sorry if I worried you. I was only thinking."

"About?"

"Oh, you know—life." She forced a laugh. "My to-do list."

Meg did not return her smile. "I think it was more than that."

"How would you know that?"

Meg leaned her head to one side. She narrowed her eyes at Priscilla. "You're kidding. Right?"

Priscilla frowned. She'd met Meg at a turning point in her life—or very near one. Though she didn't know all that troubled her friend then, she knew that Meg understood heartbreak. If what she was experiencing right now truly was heartbreak ...

"Listen, my friend"—Meg leaned close and linked her arm with Priscilla's—"you were there for me in Italy and I want to be here for you now. It's no secret that your ex showed up at the hotel unannounced—at least from what Trace said it was unannounced."

Priscilla gasped a little, her mouth hovering open as she thought of words to fill it.

Meg patted her arm. "Trace has a good heart. You know that. But nothing gets past her."

"It's true. Leo showed up with his daughter, Mia. I, of course, had no idea they were coming."

Meg's eyebrows pulled closer together. "That must have been very hard for you. What did he want?"

Her gaze focused on the neatly kept path. "He wanted me."

"Of course he did."

"I mean, he wanted me to come back home and help him raise Mia." She lifted her gaze to meet Meg's. "His new wife left him."

"Shew ... girl."

"Yes. It was quite a shock."

Meg watched her, those brows dipping low, her mouth puckered. "You didn't consider it."

Priscilla hugged herself, thinking. She took a breath and lifted her chin, squaring her eyes on Meg's. "For about two seconds."

"Oh ..."

"Mia is a darling girl." She put up a palm, like a stop sign. "No need to scold me—I won't listen, you know."

Meg's eyes opened wide and she quirked her chin to one side. "Oh, I know."

Priscilla's gaze found Meg's. "I said goodbye to him—to them. And I've made my peace with that."

"Sure you have."

A force, small but powerful, attacked one of the underlying supports that held up Priscilla's carefully constructed facade.

Her cheek, near the corner of her mouth, began to tremble. She glanced away from Meg, as if hoping to send her friend's attention elsewhere.

"If you say *c'est la vie* right now, I'll kill you."

"I'm fine."

"You are not fine! Priscilla, you're hurting. I can tell and I want to help you through this." She put a hand on Priscilla's shoulder. "Let me, okay?"

Priscilla nodded. She inhaled, steadying herself, and gave her friend a resigned look. "Want to come in for a glass of wine?"

"Absolutely I do."

Priscilla unlocked the door and tossed her keys into the nearby metal tray. She flipped on the lights, and Meg followed her inside.

"I've said it before, but this place is so … you." Meg was looking around, hands on her hip. "It's joyful—the way you usually are."

Priscilla went into the kitchen toward the counter where a sculpted hula dancer statue reigned near a wine rack. She plucked out a bottle, then padded over to the fridge and pulled a second bottle from inside. She spun around, a bottle in each hand.

"Red or white?"

"Red. Thanks."

She tucked the bottle of white back into the fridge, found a corkscrew, and opened the red, a brand of Chianti that had always reminded her of her travels through Italy. Priscilla placed Meg's glass in front of her on the square kitchen island.

"*Grazie*," Meg said.

"*Prego*."

Meg took a sip, then glanced over her shoulder. "Okay if I curl up on your couch and pull that blanket over me?"

"Of course. Please do."

When Meg was settled with a throw over her bare legs, she took another sip. "Do you still have feelings for your ex-husband?"

"No."

"Okay. Then your decision was simple."

Priscilla held her glass in the palm of her hand, a rueful curl to her mouth. "Nothing is ever very simple."

"True."

"Somehow, I knew you would understand."

"Honey, what about Wade?"

Priscilla didn't meet her eyes. "What about him?"

"The two of you looked surprisingly cozy at our pool party. I was so, so happy for the both of you—especially after what you'd both been through. Honestly, I thought, well, we all thought that you two were close to, you know, joining forces."

"You make us sound like a business arrangement."

"Forgive me. I didn't mean it that way."

Priscilla waved away any sort of offense. She slipped off her shoes and curled her legs beneath her in a big, oversized chair. "I know you didn't." She began to blink, but forced the tears away. "I thought maybe we had something special starting too," she whispered. "I haven't told that to anyone."

Meg froze, the expression on her face as fragile as Priscilla felt. "What happened?"

"He—well—darling, I just don't think the man is interested." She said those words for the second time tonight.

"That," Meg said, pointing at her. "Why do you do that?"

"Do what?"

Meg frowned. "Whenever you're about to become serious, you suddenly change directions. You make saying even negative things sound fabulous."

"You are making that up."

"I'm not and you know it."

Priscilla raked her scalp with recently manicured nails and pulled a long swag of hair down one shoulder. She sighed and pulled her phone out of her pocket, set her music app to play some soft jazz in the background, and refused to allow herself the full consumption of her feelings.

"Well," Meg said, finally, "I will say that Wade Prince is a bit of a mystery to me, to everyone, really. He can be so crazy animated when he's talking business. But ask him about himself?"—she settled into the cushions and glanced up at the ceiling—"And a lot of that chattiness disappears."

Priscilla took a sip of wine. Her mind pedaled backward to the night they had bumped into each other at the inn, after he had flown back from New York. He had practically ignored her when Sophia came upon them near the hotel's gallery. Oh, he had turned to her, but only as an afterthought. Why hadn't she told him how she felt about that when she'd had the chance?

She shook out her mane of hair again. Maybe she'd imagined the whole thing ...

"You really don't want to talk about what's bothering you?"

"I am far more confused than I ought to be right now. And that bothers me."

"Bothers you, how?"

"I should be grateful. Thankful. And I am. Truly."

Meg's gaze assessed her. "You can be both thankful and confused, you know."

"Can I?"

"You know what I think? I think you really like Wade. Maybe even love him."

Priscilla directed a poker face at Meg, noticing—but not reacting to—the look of victory on her friend's face. "I can't afford to be in love—not again. Not so soon. And not with someone who may never return those feelings." There. She said it. Did she dare look Meg's way?

"But that's the thing, my friend. You who spends her life living in the moment, you mustn't run from love, even if there's a risk of pain."

"You did."

Meg laughed and pointed her wine glass at Priscilla. "Exactly! And see where it got me?"

Priscilla gave her a what's-your-point look. "Running away got you the man of your dreams. And a pretty nice vacation, I might add."

"Fine!" Meg set down her glass. "Maybe this isn't making sense. Or maybe I just want you to realize that love is all about risks." She huffed an emphatic sigh. "Like when you ran off to Italy *all by yourself.*"

"As did you."

"We're not talking about me! I just wanted to point out that doing so was risky for you. So many untold dangers when traveling alone." Meg stopped and flipped a look at the ceiling. She frowned at Priscilla. "I'm beginning to sound like my mother."

"That's because you are one now."

Meg shook her head. "Back to my point: Your risky trip to Italy eventually led you here. And how amazing is that?"

"What makes you think I am not willing to take a risk?"

"Well, have you? I mean, since you got here?"

Something about Meg's question pricked the tender

underside of her heart. She blinked back tears, unable to fully explain why.

A few moments of silence fell between them, until Meg said, "Tell me about Leo and his little girl."

She shrugged. "Leo was, as always, selfish and handsome as all get-out." She blew out a tiny breath. "But Mia."

"Was she darling?"

Priscilla looked at Meg, eyes wide. "Yes," she whispered. "And she took to me like honey on toast." Priscilla glanced away, those tears beckoning her once more.

"That must have been hard."

Priscilla nodded, still not making eye contact.

"I'm going to ask you this one more time: Do you love him?"

"No." There was no wiggle room in her response.

Meg leaned forward, her elbows on her knees. "Have you ever grieved your marriage?" she said, eyes like lasers on Priscilla. "I mean, truly grieved the dream you once had?"

Pricilla licked her lips, discomfort needling her. "That's why I went to Italy."

Meg sat back, appearing to think deeply. "You've always been so positive about things ... *c'est la vie* and all that. But trying to lessen the pain can increase its power over you."

Those tears pressed forward, the pressure like an oncoming headache. A sob slipped out, like a naughty child, and Priscilla caught it and shooed it back inside.

"It's okay to cry." Meg laid her hand on Priscilla's knee. "You don't have to be everyone's light all the time, especially if doing so extinguishes your own. Trying to diminish the pain from your suffering can have the opposite effect, making it more potent. I did that for years with my own father's memory—maybe I'll share that with you someday."

Tears dripped freely now, down Priscilla's cheeks and off of her chin. When Leo had left, she'd been shocked. Then stoic. And then she ran away to Italy, a place she had always wanted to go. In some sense, she had been running ever since.

Conviction hit her heart. She had lectured Wade about his need for control, but had she really thought all this time that *she* was in complete control of her life?

She looked at Meg, no longer willing to hide her tears. "When I married Leo, I married for life—but there was nothing I could do to save it. Nothing. I felt like such a failure." She shook her head, overwhelmed by the searing pain that memory caused. "I had never known rejection like that, and it hurt more than I ever thought it could."

"I am so, so sorry," Meg said. "In the end, I can assure you that joy and suffering are not mutually exclusive. You can have one in the midst of the other. Do you hear what I'm saying?"

Priscilla's gaze gripped Meg's. She'd said something similar to Wade about rest and purpose.

Maybe, just maybe, it was time to take her own admonitions to heart.

CHAPTER 14

"You ladies are the best ... the absolute best!" Priscilla pulled into the center's parking lot, grateful that Meg and Liddy would take time out to join her today. EduCenter had burrowed its way into her heart and she'd become determined to help it succeed.

Meg looked out the window. A group of boys was playing basketball in the hot summer sun. "I can't believe Wade has kept this place a secret. Why do you think he'd do that?"

Priscilla thought back to her conversation with Gwynnie. "I think it had more to do with keeping his private life private." She didn't mention his wealth, though maybe they already suspected he had means to help the center.

Meg said, "Well when you blurted it out at the pool party, he didn't seem to be bothered."

Priscilla grimaced. "I would not have used the word blurted, exactly."

"Well, whatever you call it," Liddy said, "he looked pretty relieved."

Priscilla chose her words, still hyper-sensitive to the effect

Wade's current situation could soon have on the center. "The place has taken some hits recently, and I think it was weighing on him."

"What kind of hits?" asked Liddy.

"One of their biggest supporters backed out of funding."

Meg looked thoughtful. "I wonder how we can help."

Priscilla gave her friend a quick side hug. "Keep thinking like that."

"I will." Meg looked around the grounds. "Maybe the center has traditionally relied on a few big supporters, but what about starting something online?"

Priscilla tilted her head, thinking. "Like a charity?"

"Yes, charity for charity," Meg said. "Kind of a novel thought, isn't it?

Liddy clapped her hands. "Oh! Great idea. I'm surprised Wade didn't already have some kind of campaign going, like the one he did for Sophia's fashion line last year. We could even offer merch for various donations, like donate fifty dollars and get a hat, that sort of thing."

"All lovely thoughts," Priscilla said, "but I'm not so sure we want the kids to feel put on display in any way. Not that you were suggesting anything like that."

Meg nodded. "You're so sweet. Of course, you're right."

They walked into the lobby and Priscilla introduced them to Mandy while they signed in and received badges. Afterward, she led them down the hall toward the girls' lounge. "C'mon. I'll take you to my favorite spot."

"Cilla!"

Three girls rushed her, nearly knocking Priscilla over. Amber lingered behind, her expression somber. Priscilla reached out and slid an arm around her. "Hey, there, beauty. I brought some friends to meet you all. This is Meg Riley and Liddy Quinn."

They said their hellos.

Priscilla held up her toolkit. "After I give my friends a tour, I thought we could come back here so I can give Amber a new 'do and put Staci's hair into a ballerina bun."

Amber flopped onto a beanbag chair. "I don't feel like it today. You can just do her." She shrugged in Staci's direction.

Priscilla exchanged a look with Meg and Liddy. She put her toolkit on a shelf. "Maybe you'll change your mind, Amber. Do you girls want to help me give the grand tour?"

"Yeah, let's go," Staci said, leading the way.

They wandered along, passing a kitchen area, the coed lounge Priscilla admired so much on her first visit, and a couple of classrooms.

Mari jumped ahead and opened a door. "That's Wade's classroom in there, only he didn't come this week." They peeked into the room, floor-to-ceiling bookcases neatly organized, a computer area, and a cool lounge area with a massive stencil on the wall of the word: THINK.

Priscilla looked from wall to wall as the girls tumbled inside. "Has this room been remodeled recently?"

A woman's voice cut through the chatter. Candace had joined them. "That's Wade's brainchild. He came up with a plan for the students to take ownership of the room. Worked beautifully."

"Hi, Candace," Priscilla said. "The girls are giving my friends a tour. Hope that's all right with you."

"Absolutely. Any time at all!"

Meg shook her head. "I am so impressed. Truly." She turned and offered her hand to Candace. "Meg Riley."

Liddy shook Candace's hand as well. "And I'm Liddy. I'm amazed at this place, too."

"Thank you both for coming. Summer can be tough. School's out, so we're busier here than usual."

"Is there a pool?" Meg asked.

"Not yet. But"—Candace caught eyes with Priscilla for an instant—"Wade has his eye on the property next door to build one. Say a prayer he can secure it."

Liddy swung a look at Priscilla. "Does that man ever sleep?"

Priscilla turned up her palms. "Honestly, I doubt it."

"So what kind of class does Wade teach in here?" Meg asked. "How to run a successful business?"

Candace nodded. "Something like that. He teaches a Money Smart class for teens. That's actually how he became involved. One of his clients saw how good he was with finances and thought he could teach the kids some basics in a way that they could understand. His involvement grew from there."

Liddy crinkled her nose. "How often is he here?"

"Every week when he's in town, which hasn't been too often lately. The kids miss him, which is saying a lot. How many kids voluntarily attend a class in the summer?"

"Or any other time of year?" Liddy quipped.

Priscilla could relate to the kids missing Wade, even though they had parted on less-than-positive terms. He had left town shortly after she had walked out on him the other night, and she had felt the tug of his absence ever since. Then again, she had already begun the application process to become a foster parent. Did she really want to initiate something with Wade that she might not be able to fully commit to?

And, she noted with some regret, he had not called her after the abrupt end to their last conversation either.

"I have an idea," Meg said suddenly, her voice low. "What if we were to bring the kids to the inn for a short summer camp? Just brainstorming here, so bear with me. We could house about eight kids in each suite, so maybe do a boys camp, then a girls? Or a coed camp for different ages? What do you ladies think?"

Priscilla's heart melted. "I think it's an amazing idea."

"And a generous one too," Candace said.

Meg flashed a smile at Liddy. "Wanna spearhead this one?"

Liddy grinned back at her. "You know I do." She turned to Candace. "Do you have time to meet with me right now to figure out how we could pull some camps together? Maybe someplace out of earshot of the kids?"

"Absolutely."

After Liddy and Candace disappeared down the hall, Meg turned to her. "Have you given any more thought to calling Wade and patching things up?"

Priscilla shook her head. After she'd had her good cry the other night, Priscilla had confessed how she'd left things with Wade. Her friend had been nudging her to call him ever since.

Meg continued, her back toward the hall. "For what it's worth, Jackson says he's going to give it to him for being so ornery with you."

Priscilla opened her mouth to protest, then shut it quickly as she noticed Amber wandering down the hall toward them. Priscilla reached out and slid an arm around the girl's shoulder, her heart aching at the expression on Amber's face. "Hi there. Ready for your new 'do?"

Amber shrugged. "Nah. I'll watch you put that bagel in Staci's hair, though."

Staci darted up from the couch and charged toward the door. "It's not a bagel! It's a donut."

Amber frowned. "Whatever."

Mari rolled her eyes, steam forming in her expression. "You're being a brat." She swung a look at Staci. "When's Morgan getting here already?"

"All this talk about food is making me hungry," Meg said, obviously trying to diffuse the situation.

"Perfect. I've got dark chocolate in my purse." Priscilla opened her bag for all the girls to see. She reached in and pulled out a handful of wrapped truffles.

Suddenly, all hint of animosity was gone. The girls walked on ahead of Meg and Priscilla, eating their truffles and chattering as usual.

Meg laughed, watching after them. "You're a miracle worker."

"Good," Priscilla said. "Because I kind of feel like I need one of my own."

"Why's that?"

Priscilla stared at Meg for a beat. Then she pulled her into her confidence. "I have to move."

Meg shrank back. "Move? Why?"

"My condo is too small. My social worker tells me I will need another bedroom before I can be approved to be a foster parent."

"Oh no. You still have time left on your lease, don't you?"

"Unfortunately, yes. The good news is I've found another unit in our complex that might become available soon, although ..."

"Although?"

"It's quite a bit pricier." She shook her head and put a resolute smile on her face. "But that's where faith comes in, doesn't it?"

Meg set her chin. "We'll help you with whatever you need. All you have to do is ask." Her eyes bored into Priscilla's. "You need to tell Wade what you're planning, don't you think?"

Priscilla thought about that. Her heart constricted. In a perfect world, she and Wade might have pursued this scenario together, talked through all the details and requirements as a team. But that was not how things stood between them, not at all how things had been left. Ultimately, Priscilla knew she would not push Wade to accept the decision that she alone had made—despite how she felt about him.

The truth was, she had made the decision to pursue foster parenting on her own. And it very well might stay that way.

CHAPTER 15

One week later

WADE STUCK his cellphone into his suit pants pocket, glad to put away business, even if only for a short while. He and his partners were still in a holding pattern on the New York project because a small house with an indecisive owner held all the power. One firm *no* from him and the entire development—and his building sale—could be canceled. Or delayed indefinitely.

He walked the path toward EduCenter, grateful for the time he would soon have with some of the kids—something to keep his mind off the pending project. Not to mention it gave him an excuse to avoid the inn today. Jackson had called a couple of times. "Nothing urgent," he had said. So Wade had taken that as a reason not to return the call anytime soon.

He glanced around the building where boys were hanging out on the hot pavement, most of them lying on the basketball court in the corner where some shade had gathered. "Hey, Wade," one of them called.

He grinned and tossed a wave back.

Summer had brought an influx of kids, especially those with nothing else better to do. It didn't bother him one whit that his class was a take-it-or-leave-it kind of thing. He hoped that by the end of summer, those kids would slay it where money matters were concerned. That each one would understand compound interest, investing, and a variety of banking and savings terms that would surely cause them to rise above their counterparts someday soon. He hoped that each and every one of them would gain a sense of freedom from the knowledge he would do his best to impart to them.

Planning for this session of his class helped him not to dwell on his last date—if it could be called that—with Priscilla. He swallowed, trying to keep his head in the moment, his focus on the here and now. Unfortunately, his mind kept shooting back to the look on Priscilla's face that night.

If she had not been tempted to take Leo back then, she could be now.

He buried his thoughts, focusing instead on the lesson he had planned and the anecdotes he would likely share when their attentions strayed.

"You're here!" Candace called out to him when he arrived. Her face was flushed, her blonde hair windblown and slightly disheveled. "It's been so busy! The public pool closed after some weird bacteria was found in it. We have air conditioning, so we've suddenly become very popular!"

Wade sneaked a look over her head into his classroom, which was full. He flashed her a smile. "More victims for me to teach. I can't say that I'm too unhappy about that."

"Really?" Relief showed on her face. "Wade, you are the most wonderful man." She rose on her tiptoes and kissed his cheek just as Amber walked down the hall.

The teen rolled her eyes at Wade and slowed to a stop, crossing her arms in front of her bare midriff.

"Hello, Amber," he said, once Candace had rushed off to solve her next catastrophe.

"Priscilla's not here. In case you're wonderin'."

Her pronouncement, and the churlish way in which she delivered it, stopped him short. He swallowed back a reply, his eyes instinctively darting toward the far end of the hall where the girls' lounge door stood open.

"She came the other day, though."

"I see."

Amber snapped her gum, glaring at him. "Spent the whole day here doing hair and brought her friends with her."

"Have I done something to offend you, Amber?"

She shook her head, her eyes rolling upward. "Men." She unfolded her arms, dropped them at her sides, and walked past him and into the ladies room.

He screwed up his mouth. He'd seen plenty of sass from Amber, but never directed at him. He glanced down the hall, wondering if Priscilla, too, had experienced Amber's wrath. As he stood with one foot pointed toward his own classroom door and the other toward the girls' hangout, the bathroom door creaked back open.

"You acted like such a jerk the other day, by the way. I heard all about it," Amber said as she swept by. This time she didn't stop to glare at him.

"Hey, Mr. Prince?" Joaquin, the youngest of his recruits, poked his head out into the hall, a grin from one side of his face to the other.

Wade turned, though his mind was still working through Amber's chastisement.

"I'm here to collect my money," Joaquin said.

Wade nodded, his mind brought to the present. He knew exactly what Joaquin was talking about. "And you cleaned and rearranged the bookshelf?"

"Yes, sir."

Wade smiled and gestured for Joaquin to head back inside the classroom. "Let's have a look, shall we?"

They entered the room that had been in disarray for weeks, ever since a sponsor, Melody O'Leary, had died and left the contents of her storage shed to the center, stirring up all kinds of speculation.

"Maybe it's full of hats," Reed, one of the adult volunteers, had said. "Or pillows. Ladies like a lot of pillows."

"I think there're dead bodies in there," Bryce, another student, said.

Some volunteers eventually took a group of the boys to clean up the shed. And most of what Mrs. O'Leary had left for the classroom had been a perfect fit. The rest had been sold.

The question then became how to move the items in and make room for them in the large classroom. Wade wanted the kids to take ownership of the center, to treat it like their own and pass it down to each succeeding generation. That meant, if it was a mess—clean it up. If new items arrived, make room for them and gently discard what did not work.

So he had made the kids a proposal: He would offer to pay them each ten dollars for their work. However, if they invested the money by leaving it with him for two weeks, he would pay them twelve dollars instead.

Wade put a hand on his hips. He whistled sharply as he

looked around the room, which looked even better than he could have imagined. "I am impressed with all of you."

"Great." Joaquin held his palm out. "Pay up."

Several of the students cracked up, calling for their own payments.

Wade laughed. "All right. You're right. Line up and I'll pay you all your wages."

An hour later, Wade stepped out of the classroom door, his wallet—and heart—lighter. The kids had a new room that they had created with their own hard work, and they had learned the power of investing—and learning to wait.

His phone had been buzzing for the past twenty minutes, but he didn't care. The kids' reception to his lesson stirred up deep satisfaction within him.

"Wade?" Candace called out to him. "Can I have a minute before you go?"

"Sure." He pivoted away from the exit and stepped inside Candace's office.

She shut the door, her expression serious. "I'm sure you know why I stopped you."

He searched his mind for any remnant of a conversation they may have had lately. "You'll have to forgive me, Candace. It's been a long week. Were you expecting an answer from me about something?"

She shook her head. "I was talking about Priscilla's application."

"Her application."

Candace cocked her head. "You know, to foster Amber?" She stared at him for a beat. "You didn't know."

He kept his expression neutral. "I had not heard about it, no. But I have been out of state, you understand."

"Yes, of course." She stuck a fist into her hip and steadied her eyes on him. "It's just I thought, well, maybe I imagined this, but you and she are together, yes?"

"Together?"

Candace put her hand to her temple. "As in ... dating?"

She couldn't have sounded more sarcastic if she had tried, but he wouldn't give her the satisfaction of taking him by surprise. "I prefer not to discuss my personal life here."

She frowned and stuck a form into his hands. "Fine. Forgive me for prying, but it would be very helpful if you filled out this recommendation form on Priscilla's behalf. I'm trying to get her fast-tracked as an emergency caretaker for Amber."

He eyed her. "And she is agreeable to this."

"Yes. Well, she knows about the fast track, but not that I am approaching you about it." She paused. "I had thought that was a given."

"I see. What has happened to Amber's living situation?"

"It's a long story, but she had to leave quickly." Candace raised her chin. "She is currently staying with me, but once Priscilla becomes approved—she'll have to take a class and go through an inspection—then Amber should be free to move in with her."

She held the pen out and he eyed it, a thought striking him, nearly drawing blood. How long had Priscilla been considering this? Had she wanted to tell him? Worse—had she tried? Trust had not been Wade's strong suit, not in a long, long while. He had made it his business to get every agreement in writing, unsure if a person's word was enough.

Guilt wormed its way through him. He had used his past hurts as an excuse not to trust again. And where had that gotten him?

Wade looked again at the pen in Candace's hand. He took

it, signed the form giving Priscilla his highest recommendation, and handed it back to her. "You'll let her know that I took care of this?"

Candace nodded. "Sure thing,"

Then he turned on his heels and headed toward the exit, his mind reeling.

∼

AFTER PUNCHING his pillow for the umpteenth time, Wade got out of bed and headed for his office down the hall. For the next two hours, he answered emails, including one from the broker handling the sale of the building he co-owned in New York, and a handful from states outside of California's time zone. He reviewed the schedule that Laura had organized for him. And he glanced down the hall more than once, wondering if he could coax more sleep out of himself.

When the sun began lighting up his window shades, he sighed, knowing sleep was lost. At least the dreary fog that had returned to the area recently had decided to sleep in too. He sent off one last email to Laura, and hit the shower.

An hour later he strolled into the inn to meet with the chef, who was relatively new to the property. He checked his watch. Wade could only afford to give the man a half hour of his time before he had to get onto Pacific Coast Highway. He had a meeting in Santa Monica in the early afternoon and hoped tourist traffic wouldn't clog up the highway too much.

"Wade," Jackson called out. "Hang on a second."

Wade shook his hand. "Will you be joining our meeting in the kitchen? It's going to be brief."

"No, but I'm walking that way," Jackson said. "I'll join you now."

They walked on, shoulder to shoulder, Jackson unusually quiet. When the kitchen office door was in sight, Jackson turned. "I gotta ask, man. What's going on with you and Priscilla?"

Wade frowned. "You too?"

"I care about you, man."

"Thank you, but with all due respect, I prefer to keep my private life just that."

"I've noticed." He paused. "Though if you ask me, proposing to Sophia in full view of everyone doesn't exactly say private."

"So if we're done here ..."

"The ex checked out with a metaphorical bruise under his eye." He paused, chuckling. "One of the staff overheard her clocking him with her well-delivered words."

When Wade didn't answer, Jackson spat out a scoff. "She didn't go with him, man, but I'm sure you knew that. Or could have guessed that."

Wade stopped and pivoted on his heels. He kept his poker face on. "I don't know what you're talking about." Of course he knew she did not go with him—she'd met him for a drink, one that hadn't gone very well. But he wasn't about to divulge all that to Jackson.

Jackson grinned, his eyes like arrows pointing straight at Wade. "Liar."

"May I remind you, Jackson, that this isn't high school." Even as he said it, he recalled Priscilla's joke about high school never being over and had to hide the beginnings of a smirk.

"Then stop acting like it is and go talk to her." Jackson put a hand on Wade's shoulder, like he was a son speaking to his father. Or maybe older brother. "Take it from someone who's been there."

Wade could feel the tension rising in his back, as if his spine were thickening. Time was slipping by. The chef awaited him, the deal in New York could very well be disintegrating, and he still had a long drive down Pacific Coast Highway ahead of him. He raked a hand through his hair, stopping mid-rake. Jackson was staring at him, that insidious smile on his face.

"Knock it off," Wade said.

"You know you want to," Jackson said.

Silence.

Jackson chuckled. "Fine. Don't answer me, but I'm telling you, man, get her in your life and she'll keep you sane. She'll keep the crazy seas of your life smooth. Just when you think you can't take another minute of this angry world, she'll make you laugh. Then she'll make you dinner—and you'll want to serve it to *her*. Don't screw this up."

"You done, Romeo?"

"Only if I've gotten under your skin."

She's getting under my skin. Those words had pierced his thoughts the day he'd swam with her at the Riley's pool party. She'd cast a spell on him that day, and every day since, if he were honest. And yet, he had done all that he could to push her away. He'd questioned her. Challenged her. Made her get up from the table the last time they were together and walk away from him even before she had finished her wine.

His jaw clicked as his wretched behavior came into view.

Maybe the way things were left was for the best. She didn't deserve someone like him. Priscilla needed someone to live life as one big grand adventure, not a guy who lived and breathed the next deal—and brooded when life did not turn his way.

"Incidentally, did you know she and Meg met yesterday to plan a camp for the kids you've been teaching?"

"Incidentally?" He shut his eyes for a moment, letting that sink in. He snapped them open and shook his head. "I had not heard about that."

"They met out there most of yesterday afternoon." He shot a look out toward the sunny patio abutting the inn. "A whole group of them—Priscilla, Meg, Liddy—even saw Trace over there at one point. And I think Sophia popped over with designs for special camp wear."

"That's—that is a fascinating idea. Of course, I will make sure you are compensated, Jackson."

Jackson's eyes darkened slightly. "You don't understand. The camp is a gift. Priscilla let Meg know of the need, and you know my wife—she found a way to fill it. She and Priscilla are cut from the same cloth, as they say."

Wade stood there, dumbfounded. Jackson spoke about their idea, their gift, as if it were a simple proposition. He knew it was not. And yet, they set about doing it anyway.

"You've saved us, Wade. Been here for us when we needed you most," Jackson said, his expression earnest. "Let us help you with this charity that obviously means so much to you."

Jackson's kind words struck him, rendering him agitated. Priscilla had urged him to tell others about the center's needs, but his stubbornness had won out. He wanted to handle things himself. What had he been trying to prove? That he would not—could not—fail? He clenched his jaw. Unfortunately, there were no guarantees about that.

Jackson continued. "Now getting back to Priscilla, I know it was hard on you when it didn't work out with Sophia."

Wade flicked a glance at him. "That was for the best."

Jackson pressed his mouth into a line and nodded.

"Agreed. But this is different. Priscilla is different—she's perfect for you." His mouth broke into a grin. "Get out there and sweep her off her feet. She deserves it."

"We're speaking in clichés now, are we?"

"Whatever it takes, man. Whatever it takes."

The cement in Wade's spine began to chip away. The chef could wait, he supposed. And he could call Laura to reschedule his meeting on a deal in Santa Monica. The money from that project suddenly paled in his mind.

Jackson gestured outside with a flick of his head. "She's out there."

"Where?"

Jackson pointed toward the inn's exit. "She bought a paddle board—Meg went with her to pick one out. It's a nice one. Saw her an hour ago, heading for the harbor launch."

Wade swung his gaze toward the large windows in the hall. The sun was breaking through the morning's haze, like gold. He turned to Jackson. "Have a wetsuit I can borrow?"

CHAPTER 16

By the time Wade grabbed a pair of swim trunks from the inn's gift shop and borrowed Jackson's wetsuit—the one he kept in his office but never used—Priscilla was long gone.

Jackson had given him dutiful grief. "What do you need a wetsuit for? Be a man already."

"Just give it to me."

He'd carried it down to the launch area, still contemplating his next move. It was still early and the channel nearly deserted. A kayaker here, a stand-up paddle boarder there. No sign of Priscilla.

He glanced at the Kayak Shack, colorful kayaks lined up on the man-made beach. He took a step, then stopped. What had Priscilla said about him? That his clothes were "impossibly starched"?

He grimaced. She might as well have called him a chicken. A rack near the hut held paddle boards in varying sizes. Priscilla had actually bought one, and now she was out there, somewhere. He glanced out to see. *Sweep her off her feet,* Jackson had said.

Yeah, but what if seeing him flailing around on a board ended up being his kryptonite?

"Eh, there, brotha," the rental guy called out to him. "Help ya with something?"

He flickered a glance at the guy, his skin tan and showing slight signs of leathering. "I'd like to rent a board."

"Cool. I'm Brett." The guy moved toward the rack and pulled out a particularly long board. He called to Wade over his shoulder. "Ever do this before?"

"Nope."

He nodded like he already knew that. "This one's got an extra thick grip pad on it. Works good for beginners." He peeled a look up at Wade. "Can you swim, daddy-o?"

Wade scowled. He wasn't that old. "Of course."

"Great. Follow me." He set the board down on the sand, nose pointing toward the lapping water. Then he handed him a fanny pack.

Wade eyed him. "What's that for?"

"To keep you from drowning."

"I said I could swim." He said this through gritted teeth.

Brett laughed, a surprising, high-pitched sound. "'Course, but this is a life vest you wear around your waist. Harbor Patrol requires it for SUPs."

"Sups?"

"Stand up paddlers."

"Ah. By the way, did you happen to see a woman paddle out recently? Red hair?"

Brett whistled. "You mean Priscilla, I take it. Yup. She took off about an hour ago. Maybe less. She's a strong one."

"Hm." Wade snapped the life preserver around his waist and raised both hands. "Am I legal?"

"Yeah. I need to get your credit card first, daddy-o."

Wade whipped out payment, but pulled it back just as Brett reached for it. "Only if you stop calling me daddy-o."

"Okay ... pops."

Wade narrowed his eyes.

That high-pitched laugh again. "Just messin' with you"— He glanced at the credit card then looked back up—"Mr. Prince. And I don't think you're gonna want to wear that suit out there."

"No?"

"That one's kind of a relic, man. It's a winter suit too. Too hot today for that." He handed Wade a paddle. "Board shorts work great. Don't be shy—chicks dig a guy with pecs."

"Is that right?"

Brett laughed. "Okay, now, I set you up on the sand. Much easier than launching from those docks over there. Start on your knees, paddle out, and when you get used to the feel of that board beneath you, give standing a try." He looked up. "You're not thinking about going out into the waves, I hope?"

"Not today."

Brett nodded. "Good call."

Wade tried hard not to think about the lack of protection on the vessel he was about to climb aboard. As advised, he started on his knees, feeling perfectly ridiculous, but determined to get up on his feet before he reached the opening to the channel's wide breadth.

He stuck the paddle into the water and pulled in a downward motion, one side to the next. With each push against the water's resistance, he shoved away thoughts of work. Of appointments. And deals. And those calls he had planned to make on his drive down to his appointment later today—the appointment he had cancelled without so much as an explanation.

Usually, when he thought of his to-do list, adrenaline rose from somewhere deep in the pit of his gut. That adrenaline kept him moving forward, toward his target goals. As he continued to loft out into this area of the water, where birds soared and dove for breakfast, Wade began to shed those thoughts. His calendar, which had little-to-no whitespace available, began to drift away from his mind as sure as each stick of the paddle moved him farther away from shore.

And it surprised him, almost to the point of annoyance. Normally he would be angry at himself right now, incensed at his lack of focus on his business pursuits. He had not built his business, his bank accounts, by allowing his focus to become untethered and a part of him clung to his tried-and-true self.

If he were honest with himself, all he wanted to do right now was to unmoor himself from all that kept him tied to a daily schedule, like a line being unhitched from a cleat secured to a dock.

And the more his mind let go of the thoughts that often kept it bound, his body followed. He was floating out in the channel now, conscious of the intake and exit of his breath. Wade raised the paddle above his head and stretched, allowing fresh oxygen to filter through him, like a healing massage.

Slowly, he put a foot on the grip pad of his board. He felt steady, strong. Then the other foot, raising himself to a standing position, while holding the paddle out for balance. The breeze hit his chest, cooling him from the top of his head to the toes that gripped his board. A new kind of adrenaline surged within him.

He began to paddle more deliberately now, digging deeper into the water, reveling in its smoothness, in the progress he made with each stroke. He huffed a smile. Even out here, he found himself in competition with ... himself.

Get a grip, Prince.

He forced himself to look toward the wide expanse of sky and sea. Doing so helped him pull himself out of his own efforts and to focus on the divine. He released a sigh, this one saturated with gratefulness. He had lived here for years, had passed this very sea by on his daily drive, but how often had he experienced it?

Sadly, not often.

Priscilla, on the other hand, had embraced it all. Despite the despicable situation her ex-husband had impressed upon her and the new surroundings she'd found herself in, she had plunged forward, taking on new challenges and adventures. He pictured her on that first day that he'd noticed her. Why had he been so impolite to her at Sophia's wedding? Was he so absorbed, so myopic that he could not put aside his work for one minute to be charming to a newcomer who had approached him with such openness?

What a dolt.

Wade scanned the waters ahead, searching for a sign of Priscilla. A slight chill ran through him thinking of her being out here all by herself. As magnificent as it was, anything could happen. Had she known the rules and worn a life jacket? Would she stay safe in the harbor or venture out to the open sea?

He shuddered, hoping she would read his mind and stay

on calm waters. Though he was beginning to understand the draw of this sport, he wasn't keen on having to stay balanced on the waves—or worse—be tossed off into the water.

A whir of a nearby boat caught Wade's attention. He glanced to his left where a guy and his dog were putting along, the outboard motor creating a small wake. The guy lifted his hand in a brief wave as he passed by.

Now there's an idea. Why hadn't he rented a boat instead ...?

Wade dug his paddle into the water harder, left, right, left again, hopeful that he would find Priscilla out here somewhere. And soon. A couple of paddle boarders appeared up ahead, near the corner where he would be turning. An electric boat bounced along carrying five silver-haired women. They laughed and clinked champagne flutes that, given their bright orange color, probably held healthy pours of mimosas.

Wade reached that corner faster than he had expected, the wind carrying him along. As he did, he ushered himself into the wide main channel of the harbor where everyone had been hiding, apparently. The dense blue waters provided a playground for yachters as much as sailors, kayakers, and SUPs. He continued to slice his way through the water, though the direction of the wind had changed, offering up resistance rather than help. The closer he paddled toward the mouth of the harbor, the more tumultuous the waters became.

Nothing about this surprised him. Wade had been on boats many times, usually with clients, and had noted the traffic of all sizes on his way through the channel. For a short time, he had even owned a good-sized yacht, though he'd sold it quickly, realizing how little time he had for play. He remembered both the presence and absence of wind, seemingly fickle at times. But with this new experience, his perspective changed. He was no longer on board a seaworthy vessel with a captain at the helm, no longer felt sturdy ground beneath him. In some peculiar way, this lack of reliance appealed to Wade in a way he had not considered before.

A wolf whistle broke his thoughts. He looked to his left. Maybe "wolf" wasn't the right term. Did cougars whistle? He could not avoid the stares of the women on the tandem kayak that paddled up next to him. Try as he did.

"Hey there, sailor!" The woman who called out to him sat in the front, barely turning her paddle. She wore her dark hair piled high on her head and silver cat-eye sunglasses on her face, like she was straight out of the 1960s. "You're looking fine out here."

"Hello, ladies."

"Ooh, and so polite!"

The other woman, cheeks puffed out and red, laughed. She was paddling hard against the wind and the thought crossed his mind that he hoped she would not need medical assistance anytime soon.

As they passed him by, the first one shouted back, "How about you meet us at that inn back there for a drink later? My treat!"

He saluted them, noting how they both shrieked with laughter, but he kept his answer—a hearty "no"—to himself. The waters ahead were teeming with so many adventurers that Wade began to wonder if he would ever find Priscilla out here. Water lapped over his board and he slowed, taking it all in. A sea lion's head broke the surface of the water mere yards in front of him. The animal turned his head like a periscope, slowly and purposefully. After a minute or so, he dove downward, his bulky body splitting the water before following the rest of him into the depths.

Wade considered his options: paddle like crazy in hopes that the lion would lose interest in him or hold his ground and hope that he already had.

He chose to stay put. That's when he noticed a deep-toned bark followed by the grind of a boat engine in the distance. He snapped a look across the channel where a lone dock jutted out into the harbor, surrounded by a shore of jagged rocks. A fat sea lion, one of the largest he'd ever seen, sunned itself on the edge. Several other sea lions swam around the base of the dock, their heads breaking the surface of the water followed by flippers and tails when they dove below.

"Wade!"

He looked between the dock and saw her there, her paddle at her side. Priscilla stood tall, confident, her red hair billowing behind her. A goddess.

He went mute ... dumbstruck.

The sound of that engine grew. She shaded her eyes, a smile dancing on her face. She cupped her hand around her mouth and shouted, "I'm not sure if this harbor is big enough for the both of us."

He grinned and shouted back, "I will prove you wrong about that." Wade continued to watch her, ever aware of the raft of sea lions frolicking on just the other side of her. His pulse quickened. She drew him toward her with her light and joy, her beauty and love of adventure. How could he have become so mired in loss to not trust in what he had found?

The water turned choppy, the noise from that boat engine growing louder. He turned, noting that a sleek vessel had entered through the harbor mouth, its hull shaped liked a classic cigarette boat. Wade frowned as the boat made its way down the channel at higher speed than was allowed.

He swung his gaze back to Priscilla, aware that her smile had faded too. He shaded his eyes. She looked over her shoulder toward the approaching boat and dug her paddle into the water, turning hard toward the dock behind her. The speedboat continued toward them without slowing, its passengers' mouths open in celebratory smiles, likely oblivious to their captain's reckless behavior.

He frowned. She was trying to get out of the boat's way, but would those sea lions be open to her joining them?

All other vessels on the channel near the speeding boat had scattered. If Wade stayed put, he, too, would be out of harm's way—from what he could tell about the boat's direction—though subject to a wake that might very well upend him and his board.

Then the unthinkable—the boat turned slightly and headed straight for Priscilla. Wade waved his paddle over his head, hoping to get the speedboat captain's attention. When that didn't work, he dropped his paddle into the water and gave it a hard shove. Everything was happening so fast. He paddled harder, gulping air as he did.

Priscilla had nearly reached the dock and hovered beside it, probably staying careful not to disturb its resident. Instead of continuing down the channel, the speedboat slowed, but only slightly. Laughter punctuated the air.

"Shoo!" one of the boaters called out.

The captain continued straight for the dock, skimming it as it passed. Wade kept his eyes trained on Priscilla, who had turned her board again and paddled farther away, only to switch back again after the boat passed her, like she was trapped.

Wade cut through the center of the channel as the speedboat's engine revved. "Hey!" He held up his paddle to get the guy's attention. "Stop!"

The guy waved and shouted, "Steer clear! I'm gonna clear my dock!"

Clear the dock? Did he not see Priscilla there, trapped? That's when he realized: The boat captain was trying to scare off the sea lion that had taken up residence on his dock so he could land there.

Unfortunately, Priscilla had nearly reached the dock again. "Cilla!" Wade shouted. "Move away from the dock!" Whatever fears he'd had about being on the water had completely vanished, his mind gripped at the thought of Priscilla in the water, surrounded by sea lions. Even the gentlest of creatures could turn aggressive when their territory became threatened.

As she tried to move away, the boat once again skirted the dock. Wade groaned, and paddled faster than he thought possible just as the massive sea lion dove into the water, knocking Priscilla off her board and into the murky channel waters below.

∽

"Priscilla!"

She heard him calling out to her, her mind jostling between the shock of cold water surrounding her and the fact that Wade had showed up out here in the middle of choppy waters.

He was paddling hard toward her. Priscilla could tell by the excessive rippling of his biceps as he charged forward, digging in his paddle, determination lining his brow. Amazing what one could make out from yards away.

"There's a girl in the water!" someone shouted.

The captain of the sleek boat cut its engine and passengers scrambled to peer over the side at her.

"A girl?" the driver shouted. "Where?"

Was she that unremarkable that the boat captain had not seen her? She rolled her eyes like a teenager and made a mental note to purchase a neon yellow rash guard to wear the next time.

Wade had traversed much of the channel, sending all kinds of sparks through her as she floated there, trying to determine her next move. Forget about that daft boat captain. The one who mattered had seen her—and he was paddling this way.

"Cilla!"

"Wade." Her voice broke when she said his name, surprising even her. She clung to her board, her paddle nowhere to be found, her arms wobbling like jelly fish.

When Wade reached her, he knelt on his board. Then he reached across and warmed her hands with one of his. "When we get back to shore I'm going to wring that boat captain's neck," he muttered.

"I would buy a ticket to see that."

His gaze washed over hers.

She smiled up at him.

"Are you hurt?" he asked.

She shook her head. "Just cold. And a little scared my toes might become somebody's lunch."

A crushingly loud bark split the air. Priscilla held her breath. The big ol' sea lion that had caused her to fall off her board hoisted its well-fed self back onto the dock, causing it to groan and shudder under the animal's weight. She swung a startled look back at Wade. "He outweighs us all, I'm sure."

Wade winked. "Probably best not to think on that right now."

A voice from behind broke through. "Need some help?"

"Might have thought of that earlier, Captain," Wade muttered and swung a gaze toward the guy at the helm of that boat. He turned back to Priscilla, giving her a gentle look. "I'll steady the board. Do you think you can climb back on?"

"I cannot believe you are here." Her voice trembled, her lips surprising cold. "You are ... you're my rescuer."

Wade stared at her for a beat, concern in his eyes. He swung another look toward that boat. A woman watched them with a worried frown, her forehead knotted. She held a towel out to him. "Please. Let us help?"

He nodded. "We need a ride back to the inn."

"Absolutely," the woman said. "Get her to the stairs and we'll take you where you need to go."

Priscilla watched as he handed the woman his paddle. Then with free hands, he carefully gripped the edge of Priscilla's board and pulled her around toward the waiting boat. "I'll hold your board while you climb into the boat."

Minutes later, Wade, with Priscilla wrapped in a towel, sat on the speedboat as a remorseful captain ferried them back to the inn. She shivered and Wade cinched her closer to him. He put his warm hand on her cheek, the touch of him warming her to the core.

She turned a look up at him. "You have an anchor on your back."

"Do I?"

Priscilla took him in, his browning skin, the way his dark eyes followed her. "It's sexy."

He broke out in a grin and tightened his grip on her.

"That's quite a compliment coming from a mermaid like yourself."

She smiled broadly at this, suddenly growing warmer. Priscilla had never felt quite this safe in her entire life. "What does it mean?"

"I had it made one day in my twenties when I found myself being tossed around by uncertainty." His jaw twitched. "It was meant to remind me that strength and stability are there for the taking, that there's always something bigger holding me in place. Frankly, I had forgotten it was there."

"I'm glad you've been reminded."

He wicked a look at her. "Yeah, me too."

They sat in silence, the whir of the boat's engine the only sound between them. Finally, Priscilla spoke. "You told me that you never wanted to paddle board, that you never wanted to be prey."

"Did I say that?"

"You did."

He chuckled. "Well, then, I suppose you could say that my concerns were legitimate."

She smiled at him, yet still unsure of what it all meant. "Oh, Wade, I am so confused by you. I honestly don't know what to think right now."

"Ask me anything."

She stared at him. "Why did you come? I thought we were ... done."

He brushed strands of hair from her cheek. "I'm sorry for the way I behaved the last time together. Would you believe that I wanted to sweep you off your feet?"

"Instead I got swept off my board."

He groaned and pulled her closer. After a moment, he whispered, "Yes, and I've never been so afraid in my life."

"Really?" she said. "Even more afraid than climbing onto that paddle board in the first place? Of possibly being prey to that big ol' sea lion—or worse?"

He paused, then said, "Even more afraid than that."

"Wow," she whispered, searching his eyes. Then Priscilla lowered herself back into his embrace, nuzzling close to him beneath his chin. "Wow."

CHAPTER 17

"So you really think teenagers will enjoy a harbor cruise?" Meg was asking.

Trace put a fist to her hip. "You mean sittin' around being fed while someone else does the carting around? Yep, I think it's a great idea."

Priscilla nodded her agreement. "Oh, darling, yes. I think they'll love it. And I've already spoken with Chef and he's planning foods he thinks they'll enjoy."

Liddy picked up her phone and made some notes. "I'd better check on that. His idea of teen-friendly food might be tuna without the tartare."

Meg laughed. "Or lamb with extra mint jelly."

Priscilla laughed lightly. "Not to worry. We don't know how exotic their tastes are so I've asked him to stick with sandwiches and chips."

"And some of those fresh-baked brownies, I hope," Trace added.

Priscilla nodded. "I'll make sure to tuck an extra one in

your box, Trace. I'm so glad you've agreed to come along as a chaperone."

Trace stared at Priscilla, blinking rapidly. "I-I'm super happy you'll have me. I can't wait!"

Sophia breezed into the early morning meeting looking as if she'd fallen out of a magazine. Her hair hung loose and fresh at her shoulders, her yellow sundress showing off her tanned skin. "Good morning, ladies." She set a basket of scones on the table. "I tried a new recipe I hope you will like—cranberry-tangerine."

Her gift was met with a crescendo of *oohs.*

"Some people have a gift," Liddy said, biting into a scone. She pointed at Sophia. "You are just one of those people. Whip up a scone? Sure. Throw together a beautiful dress? Why not?"

Sophia smiled. "You are embarrassing me."

Meg broke off a piece of the decadent bread and popped it into her mouth. "Nothing to be embarrassed about, Sophia. This is heavenly. I'm so glad we're related now."

"Speaking of family," Liddy said, throwing her gaze Priscilla's way. "Have you heard from Wade about the, you know, deal?"

"Family?" Trace interrupted, pursed her lips, and looked from Liddy to Priscilla and back again. "Is there something you haven't told me yet, Priscilla?"

Heat crawled up Priscilla's neck. She and Wade had spent considerable time together over the past few weeks, but they had not discussed anything ... permanent. She wasn't sure if they ever would. "I have no idea what you're talking about, Liddy. But"—she held up her forefinger—"I know that he hopes to hear something soon. Perhaps even today."

Meg sighed. "Good. Looking forward to seeing less stress on that man's face."

"And more support for the center soon, hopefully," Liddy added.

"Yes," said Priscilla. "Hopefully."

∽

BY THE TIME the first two groups of teens arrived at the dock, Priscilla had forgotten all about the incident in the harbor several weeks prior. Well, almost. She waited to greet the campers beside a stack of life vests—though their captain had already told her they would not be required to wear them on the boat.

The girls bounded up to her with Amber leading the way. From behind, some of the boys dawdled, their hands in their pockets, their eyes guarded, while others seemed to jostle their way along, elbowing each other and becoming distracted by the other boats, the sea, and anything else that flew, splashed, or dove.

As the kids climbed aboard, Priscilla handed them each a life vest "just in case." Trace was waiting on board clad in tan shorts, a windbreaker, and a visor advertising Sea Glass Inn. Priscilla cracked a smile when she caught sight of the whistle hanging around Trace's neck.

Joaquin, one of the younger boys in Wade's Money Smart class, dawdled behind. Priscilla held a life vest out to him. "Welcome, aboard."

The boy glanced at the vest, his hands in his pockets. His stance was stiff and unfriendly, but in his eyes Priscilla saw fear. She put the vest back onto the pile and instead gestured for him to join her. She smiled. "Let me show you around. Would that be okay?"

He nodded, his eyes snapping left to right, as if surveying his surroundings.

While the rest of the kids were finding the perfect spot to sit, Priscilla led Joaquin inside the boat's cabin and up some steps where the captain was preparing to depart.

"Captain Alex, I have someone for you to meet. This is Joaquin."

Captain Alex was a burly man with curly black hair, a thick beard, and a kind smile. He reached out a hand. "Greetings, Joaquin!"

Joaquin shook the captain's hand wordlessly.

He gestured toward a woman wearing garb similar to his. "And this is my First Mate, Maria."

"Welcome, Joaquin," Maria said.

Priscilla held the captain's gaze, gesturing slightly toward the boy. Captain Alex gave her a brief nod and put his hand on the boy's shoulder. "You're going to be our Junior Captain today. The views are amazing up here—you'll be astounded!" He swung his gaze back to Joaquin. "How does that sound?"

Joaquin seemed to think about this. He swiped a tongue across his teeth and nodded. "Yeah. Cool."

As Priscilla made her way back to the main deck, relief flowed through her. Inside the cabin, the girls clumped together near a window, talking over each other. Outside, several of the boys hung over the side until Trace shooed them off the rails.

The captain called everyone out onto the deck, then gave them all a brief rundown of the rules before pushing the boat away from the dock. The captain moved slowly through the harbor and spoke through a loudspeaker to call out egrets, herons, and pelicans that hovered above the water. He also told them to watch for sea lions and bat rays that sometimes swam close to the surface.

A small sea lion poked through the water on the starboard side. "Hey," one of the boys said, "isn't that the fish that knocked you over, Priscilla?"

"He was that little?" Staci said.

Another boy said, "That little thing? I could've won him arm wrestlin'!"

"That's cuz sea lions don't have arms!" Mari said.

The first boy cracked up, which fed into a frenzy of laughter, most of it directed at Priscilla. She leaned against the railing, her arms over the side, her own laughter filling her ears. The rush of air against her skin lifted her spirit further. So much peace out here on the water, with these kids. Priscilla could honestly say, she'd found so much of what she had been searching for.

∼

Though the time had barely dipped into the afternoon, camp day number one was already going well. Wade was waiting for them as they disembarked and Priscilla tried to gauge his expression for any sign that his New York sale was no longer in jeopardy.

Unfortunately, his face was still a mask.

He kissed her swiftly, then turned to the group of boys who had straggled off the boat. "Ready for a swim?"

And ... they were off.

Liddy held up a clipboard. "Okay, ladies. We'll be meeting Priscilla and her crew in the spa soon for some fun downtime. Let's go back to your suite and change clothes, shall we?"

After the girls had disappeared, Priscilla wandered up to the salon. Katrina laughed when she saw her. "You look beat! Here"—she patted the top of an empty salon chair—"sit."

Priscilla collapsed into the chair with a high-pitched sigh. "Feels good to get off of my feet for a few minutes."

"Girl, don't give me that—you usually work in heels."

"Yes, but I don't chase teenagers around in them."

"True." Katrina called out to a woman across the room. "Frankie, we need a shoulder massage over here—stat!"

Just as she was beginning to feel a sense of revival through her nerves and muscles from the massage, Priscilla's phone rang.

"Don't answer that." Frankie pressed her thumbs harder into Priscilla's shoulders.

She let it go, but it started up again. Priscilla reached for her phone, concerned it might be her social worker. "Hello?"

"Priscilla? Oh good, it's you! This is Laura. Have you seen Wade?"

She sat up abruptly. "He's in the pool right now. Is it urgent?"

"You better believe it is. I must find him immediately. Will you have him call me?"

"Of course." She stood, looking for her shoes. "I'll go out to the pool and have him call you from there."

Priscilla dashed out to the pool, slowing as she approached. If she could, she would have stood and watched him from the shadows a little longer. Wade was sitting on the edge of the pool, shirtless, his legs dangling over the side. He appeared to be refereeing a water volleyball match, his muscles flexing in response to the game's activity.

Her knees weakened, as did the rest of her. Priscilla caught her breath, keenly aware of the message she had to deliver, and regretting how doing so would disrupt the idyllic picture she was walking into.

Wade's face lit up when he first caught sight of her, but that high-wattage smile dimmed when she said, "Laura wants you to call her. She says it's urgent."

He looked at her for a beat then turned toward the lifeguard tower. He put his thumb and forefinger into his mouth and caught the guard's attention with a whistle. "Take over for me, will you?"

Before he left, Wade cupped Priscilla's chin and kissed her soundly. Then he left in a hurry.

CHAPTER 18

Amber pushed off from the shore, her paddle board gliding quickly away from everyone else. She threw a shout over her shoulder to Priscilla. "You think this fog's ever gonna let up?"

"Darling, we're going to enjoy this day, fog or not."

Behind them, Gwynnie knelt on her paddle board. "I like this weather. Not too hot." She paddled to keep up. "Reminds me of the Pacific Northwest. Very mysterious."

Priscilla laughed. "Ah, mysterious. A wonderful way to put it!"

"Hey, wait for us!" Sadie's tiny voice piped up from the shore.

Priscilla turned her board around and shaded her eyes, watching as Wade strapped the little girl into a life jacket before she climbed into a bright yellow kayak.

Amber slowed too. "Can't believe your boyfriend's goin' old school on that yak."

Priscilla laughed. "The old softie!" When she first met Wade, she couldn't imagine ever calling him that. He was direct, not quick to smile, and had an evil eye for days—one sexy, evil eye.

Then again, perhaps those qualities had helped him succeed. Though the New York deal had dipped and climbed like a roller coaster, in the end, the property sale went through. Her mind replayed the thrill of hearing the news.

"It's done," he said that first night of camp, after all the kids had gone to sleep.

"Darling, such wonderful news!"

He pulled her into an embrace and she peered up at him. "You were worried?"

"I was ... concerned. However, I never let them see a drop of sweat." Wade leaned his forehead against hers. "Priscilla, the sale is complete and an exchange is in process."

"Exchange?"

"Yes. I have already reinvested the funds into commercial property on this coast."

"Wait. So you've bought another building?"

He rubbed his thumb over the corner of her downturned mouth. "Don't worry. I have reinvested the profit to defer paying taxes on capital gains. This has allowed me to invest in property that, in this case, already generates millions in rental income."

"I have no idea what any of that means."

"It's good news." He kissed her, more slowly than in the past, as if staking his claim. She rested her hand on his dress shirt, palpably aware of the hardness of his chest beneath the fabric.

She tilted her head up, meeting his gaze. "You remind me of the cover of a bodice ripper."

"Bodice ripper?"

"You know, those romance novels with a billionaire on the cover,

the buttons of his starched white shirt undone to here." She demonstrated, playfully.

Wade leaned his head back at that, his laughter a quiet roar. "No, I didn't know, but thank you for filling me in. Everything you said is about right—except the starch."

Priscilla stilled. She flicked her gaze to his eyes. "Wait. Does this mean you've earned your billionaire status?"

A slow smile stretched across his face then ... and he kissed her into silence.

PRISCILLA'S MIND returned to where she and the others waited out on the water. The three of them—Amber, Gwynnie, and Priscilla— floated along as Wade gave his kayak a brief push from the shore and jumped in. The boat rolled side to side and Sadie screeched. But Wade deftly pulled her onto his lap, grabbed his paddle, and pushed their boat hard off of the sand. He glided toward them, his smile triumphant.

"We ready?" Priscilla asked.

Amber dug her paddle into the harbor water. "Let's do this already."

"Woohoo!" Gwynnie said, still in a kneeling position on her board. "This is so much fun!"

"So embarrassing." Amber wagged her head back and forth.

It was almost too much. Priscilla stood tall, reveling in the sea air's embrace, unconcerned with the way it tied tendrils of her hair in knots. It had been too long since she had traversed these waters. After her scare last month, she'd planned to "get back on her board" right away. But life grew crazy. Meetings and classes to attend. Meals to cook. People to care for.

She wouldn't change a thing.

"Hey, beautiful."

She glanced over her shoulder, a smile edging on her face. Wade had reached her, looking both sexy and paternal, with Sadie's fingers digging into one of his arms as he gripped the paddle that moved them forward.

"Hey, yourself." She grinned at the little girl in his lap. "What do you think, Sadie?"

"I love it! Go faster Uncle Wade, go faster!"

Priscilla winked at him. "I'll try to keep up—just don't go over the speed limit or you might find yourself in hot water."

His eyebrows raised, presenting a challenge. "Race you to the dock where I rescued you?"

She clucked her tongue. "Darling, you mean the place where I *let* you rescue me."

He threw back a laugh, those dark eyes of his still trained on her. "So that's how we're going to play it."

"Uncle Wa-de, go faster!"

Gwynnie groaned as she floated on her paddle board nearby, trying to push herself up into a standing position. "Stop bossing your uncle around, young lady!"

Amber had already pulled out far in front, so Priscilla gripped her board hard with her toes and dug in her paddle, chasing after the teen. Her biceps flexed with each pull against the water, her breathing surprisingly choppy. She glided alongside Amber, thankful to have caught up with her when she had.

"Pretty soon you're not going to want to do this with me," Priscilla said with a laugh, clearly winded.

Amber stood still, her board pointed toward the main channel, which was already delivering small, wind-driven waves from the open sea. Her strawberry-blonde hair played on the wind behind her, but she didn't flinch or say a word.

"Amber?"

A tear ran down the side of the girl's face and she flicked it away, sniffling once.

"What's wrong?"

Amber shrugged in her usual way. "Nothin."

Priscilla set her gaze on the water where birds hovered, looking for lunch. She inhaled, allowing the fresh air to fill her. "You know, I cried on a boat a few months ago. We were heading out to sea and a pod of dolphins started showing off. Really took my breath away."

"That's weird."

Priscilla bit her lip, slightly exasperated. "I'm just saying it's okay to cry when you see something beautiful. God gave you a tender heart. Nothing wrong with that."

Amber stayed quiet, but more tears began to fall faster than she could flick them away.

Priscilla grew concerned. "Honey, is something else bothering you?"

"I-I just don't want it to end."

For a brief second, Priscilla looked out at the foggy sky and measured in her mind how long she thought they would stay out today. She'd planned this excursion for all of them a week ago and had hoped for blue skies, but alas, it wasn't meant to be. She had no thoughts of canceling, though, nor shortening their adventure for she had learned that life had a way of upending her plans anyway. She reached over and patted Amber's shoulder, careful not to knock them both over.

As her hand touched the young girl's shoulder, she realized where she'd been wrong. Amber was crying openly now, the sound and picture of it ripping at her insides until her heart began to tug at her, aching. She shook her head and whispered, "I have no plans to end anything, Amber."

Amber shook off her tears and turned away, using her paddle to keep her balance. "I've heard that before."

Priscilla heard Sadie's squeals behind her. She glanced back to see Wade paddling the kayak toward them with Gwynnie struggling to stay upright next to him and Sadie. His smile stilled. *Everything okay?* he mouthed.

She nodded, though her smile took effort. Amber began to pull away, digging in her paddle and gliding away faster now.

"How come we going slow, Uncle Wade?" Sadie looked truly concerned about their lack of speed. "Is our boat broken?"

Wade gave her a comical wink. "We don't want to leave Priscilla alone, now, do we, Sadie?"

Priscilla flashed him a fake laugh. "I beg your pardon?"

Sadie peered up at her. "You have to go slow, Pa-cilla?"

Priscilla gazed at Wade, still aware of Amber's distance and keeping an eye on her the best she could. He was so ... gorgeous. His dark hair, salted in spots, framed piercing eyes that she'd found she could lose herself in. Watching him with his precious niece was like seeing a muscle builder holding a puppy—he was strong yet doting at the same time. She very well could lose her mind if she stayed focused on him too long ...

"It looks like Amber's going rogue on us." He gestured toward the teen who had gone on ahead of them. "Should we be concerned?"

A sliver of sunshine had wrestled its way through the cottony fog, sending hope of blue skies ahead. If she'd had her camera with her, Priscilla could post a photo of Amber and her board on social media as an ad for stand-up paddle boarding.

They'd make a mint.

But Priscilla had learned that making money and living a full life had little to do with one another.

Priscilla threw a look over her shoulder at Wade. "I'll go catch up with Amber. Can y'all meet us at that infamous dock?"

Gwynnie gasped. "The one with the sea lion the size of Sasquatch?"

Priscilla tried not to laugh too hard. She knew the likelihood was slim that the same sea lion still resided there. "That's the one!" She took off after Amber, eager to finish their conversation.

Priscilla paddled hard, grateful with each stroke for health, for ability, and for the adventure that each day brought. The fog was clearing, indicating midday had nearly arrived. Even so, a kind of fog had infiltrated her mind and she would not rest until it had cleared once and for all.

"You're going to have to cut me some slack!" Priscilla pulled the paddle hard against the tide, grateful that she'd finally caught up with the teen. "I think my biceps are cramping up."

Amber gave her a droll look. "You have biceps?"

"Ha ha ha."

The teen slowed some, as if she wanted Priscilla to catch up with her. Priscilla's heart began to race, but she licked her lips, took in a deep breath, and pushed forward. "I want to ask you something, Amber."

Amber peeked over her shoulder. Priscilla saw anxiety residing there, but she also saw resolve. And a hint of affection. "Yeah?"

"Let's sit."

Amber's brows knit together. "On our boards?"

"Why not? Kind of like our own oasis out here." Carefully Priscilla lowered herself to the grip pad on her board and balanced the paddle on her lap.

Amber rolled her eyes in fitting teenage fashion, but she dutifully followed Priscilla's lead.

They sat across from each other, each on a board, riding the loll of the surf. Priscilla could see Wade and Gwynnie keeping their distance. She swung a look back at Amber. "Tell me the real reason you were crying today."

The teen scowled, but Priscilla held her gaze. Amber snapped a look at her. "Fine. I just"—she shrugged—"wanted, you know, to not have to move again."

Priscilla reached out to her. "Have I said anything to you to make you think that you'd have to?"

She pouted, picking listlessly at the grip pad on her board. "No. But I always have to."

Priscilla stilled the girl's hand with her own. "Look at me."

Slowly, Amber lifted her gaze until her eyes met Priscilla's. In them Priscilla saw the dawning of hope and the future that she'd always longed for. Tears of her own began to flow freely. "Your home is with me now, Amber," Priscilla said, squeezing the young girl's hand. "For as long as you'd like it to be."

∽

MEG AND GWYNNIE blocked Wade's view. The women were bent over a glass case peering at diamond rings presented on velvet as Wade jostled to see the offerings.

The elderly man in the impeccably tailored suit who stood on the other side of the counter cast Wade a sympathetic look.

His name tag read *Javier*. He slid his gaze to the women admiring rings. "Perhaps the gentleman would like to take a closer look?"

Gwynnie grabbed her brother by the arm, pulling him between them. "Come in here already—these are gorgeous!"

Wade examined the rings, each one creative, bold, beautiful, adventuresome—and brave. The words he had used to describe Priscilla when asked.

"Here we have a princess cut," Javier said, pointing to the fat, square solitaire. "Over here, an ivy scroll in white gold, and here is a spectacular pear-shaped two-carat diamond."

Meg shook her head. "No woman wants to be associated with anything pear shaped. Trust me on this."

Javier looked to Wade, his brows raised in a question.

"That one will be a definite no," Wade said.

Javier nodded once, put the ring away, and quickly replaced it with an equally monstrous-sized ring.

The round three-carat solitaire drew a gasp from Gwynnie.

"Why do I feel as if I am on an episode of the *The Bachelor*?" Wade quipped.

"Well, those guys *are* all rich," Meg said.

Gwynnie tapped her forefinger on her chin. "Which leads me to a question, brother dear. How come you don't live in a mansion?"

He raised an eyebrow.

Meg laughed. "Something tells me that once Priscilla says yes, he'll be putting that tract house on the market."

"Yeah," Gwynnie said, her voice dreamy, "she's a goddess. I can't imagine her living in that bachelor pad."

Wade stuck a hand on his hip. "I beg your pardon?"

Meg quirked a look at him. "It is kind of, um, brown in

there. Don't get me wrong—that's some pretty expensive brown decor you've got in your home, but our Priscilla is more of a chic whitewash-and-glass type of gal." She gave him a quick side hug. "Don't worry, my friend, she'll set you straight."

Wade exhaled. This simple trip to choose a diamond for Priscilla had taken several turns he had not expected. He made a mental note to call his real estate agent. Perhaps a stager would be in order. And would there be time for him and Priscilla to choose a new home while planning a wedding? Where would she prefer to live? He would certainly have to include Laura in his plans, as she controlled his calendar ...

"Sir?" Javier's gaze held a question.

Wade brought his mind to the present. He ran his gaze across the rings on velvet, looking for the one that had "life," but nothing quite said *Priscilla* to him. He shook his head. "I would like to see everything you have."

"Yes, sir." Javier slid the rings back into the case. Then he began unlocking case doors and pulling out rings. Just as Javier reached inside another case, Wade said, "I found it."

Meg cooed. "Oh, Wade, it's gorgeous."

"Oh my word ..." Gwynnie said. "It's perfect in every way."

Javier's face lit. "A beautiful choice, sir."

"And this one, too." Wade pointed to a much-slimmer version of the ring he had chosen for Priscilla.

"Look at that," Gwynnie said. "So rich he can buy two and decide which one to give her later."

Meg laughed raucously now. "That is pretty disgusting, Wade."

Wade shook his head, giving them both a half-hearted warning look. "You two are incorrigible."

On the drive home, with the rings safely in Wade's pocket, his mind soared. This decision was the best one he had made in a long, long while. Of course, she would have to say yes.

"What if the weather doesn't cooperate?" Gwynnie, riding shotgun, suddenly asked.

Meg cut in. "Fall is one of the clearest times out here. Besides, any night on the beach is a good night."

"True," Wade said.

"But she does love the stars," Meg added.

"Yeah, I hope the weather app isn't lying." Gwynnie shot a look over her shoulder at Meg who sat in the backseat. "Should we make sure she has her nails done first?"

Wade frowned. "Why would you ...?"

"For the pictures," Gwynnie said, emphatically. "You do have a photographer lined up, don't you? C'mon, brother. You're slipping!"

"I wouldn't worry about Priscilla's nails. She's a hairstylist, so they're always pristine." Meg shot out a laugh. "Though something tells me she would keep them that way even if she didn't have a career that displayed her hands so openly."

"You ladies are making me nervous."

Meg put her hand on his shoulder. "You have nothing to worry about. I promise you."

Wade gripped the steering wheel and drew in a breath, letting it out slowly as the world sped by. If he weren't at the helm of this car, he would be at home pacing. Like a lion. Perfection wasn't his strong suit—take his love life, for example. But tonight he wanted perfection—for her. She deserved it.

In his head, he could hear Jackson saying, *Good luck with that.*

Wade had done this once before, he reminded himself—

and failed. But this time was different. His heart was at stake more than ever before. Everything he had built until now suddenly paled. He pictured Priscilla's beautiful eyes gaping up at him those months ago in the harbor after she had fallen, her face framed by hair made a deeper shade of red by the drenching of sea water.

And Wade knew this: He would marry Priscilla even if he only had twine for rings.

∼

PRISCILLA ROLLED a second coat of sea glass green on Amber's bedroom wall, her fingers red and tired from gripping the wooden handle. But considering painting had been the last thing on her mind when she'd awoken today, she couldn't help but be impressed with their progress.

She and Amber had been lazy this Saturday morning. School had begun—a new one for Amber—and so they had indulged in some downtime in their new place, the one they'd moved into in a hurry and had still to decorate. They had eaten toast and yogurt on her comforter and watched a home improvement show while still in their PJs.

But when they got to a segment on redoing a teen's room, Amber shot up. "Can we paint my room, Mom?"

Priscilla could have said *no*—or maybe *not today*. But how could she refuse that earnest face? Besides, she'd called her *mom*.

The past few months they'd built a trust that she treasured. She knew Amber did too.

Priscilla stood back and admired the job they had done. The bluish-green color that brightened the room now would be perfect for those gray days that happened without warning on this part of the coast. "Good call on this color, dear one."

Amber giggled and pointed at her. "Oh my gosh! You have paint *all* over you!"

Priscilla twisted her mouth and glanced at her hands. Flecks of paint, like stars, covered them. She wondered if the non-toxic body wash in her shower would be enough to tackle this unexpected body art.

Her phone rang. Amber grabbed it and held it out to her. "Wade's calling you. Want me to tell him your hands are too paint-y right now?"

She laughed, shaking her head. The first thing he'd say is, *Why didn't you let me hire someone to paint the room for you?* Generous man, that one.

"Hey." She tried to keep the laugh out of her voice.

"Hi. You busy?"

She bit her lip, sliding a glance at Amber. She held a finger up to her lips and smiled. "Not too busy for you."

Amber's phone rang too, so she plopped onto the floor, laying on her back.

Wade's voice pulled Priscilla back to him. "Take a walk with me tonight?"

Priscilla leaned into the sound of the soft yet husky voice she had fallen for—she loved everything about it. She would love nothing better than to walk with Wade tonight, but she couldn't leave Amber alone. Not at night. She sneaked a look at the teen who laid on the floor, phone in her ear, a reminder of her own childhood.

Amber caught her attention. "Mom?"

Priscilla placed her hand over her phone. "Yes?"

"Gwynnie wants to know if I can help her with Sadie tonight. Can I? Please?" Gwynnie had relocated to the area and Priscilla could not have been happier to gain a new friend.

How perfect was this?

She nodded. "Of course. If you help me clean up this mess first."

Amber cracked up. "Yeah, I will."

Priscilla returned to her conversation with Wade. "A walk would be perfect."

He chuckled. "What kind of mess do you ladies have to clean up?"

She glanced at her hands, evidence of a busy day on them. "Oh, you know, the usual."

"Well, perhaps you will have to tell me tonight what 'the usual' entails."

At twilight, after Gwynnie had picked up Amber, Wade showed up at her door wearing dark jeans and a baby blue shirt that outlined his muscular body. She pulled her gaze away, restraint becoming more and more difficult.

Wade assessed her with one long stroke of his gaze. She wore a lacy white cover-up over a red sundress and her waves loose and free. "You look ... perfect."

He held out his hand and she took it. Together they made their way along the curvy path that led to the long sandy beach outside of her complex.

"Oh look at that sky!" She couldn't temper her smile, nor did she care to. Swaths of pink and gold stretched for as long and wide as they could see.

Wade wrapped his arms around her as they watched the sun drop into the ocean, the colors of the sky melding together until darkness fell.

"Your hands are cold." He turned her around gently, examining her hands finally. "Is that ... paint?"

She bit her bottom lip. "I got as much of it off as I could, but yes. It's sea glass green, in case you were wondering."

He quirked a look at her, his gaze quizzical. "Does this have something to do with the mess you and Amber had to clean up?"

Priscilla reached up and looped her hands around Wade's neck. "Darling, she asked me if we could paint her room and I had no choice but to say yes."

He nodded, grinning. "Uh-huh. You had no choice."

She flashed him a smile. "You smell wonderful, by the way."

"How come it feels like you are trying to deflect?"

"You are so suspicious!" Her arms were still looped around his neck. She dropped her head back, laughing.

He leaned his forehead against hers. "You are a mystery to me, you know that?"

She grinned and closed her eyes, their foreheads touching, a light breeze wrapping them. They swayed there together, the breeze carrying them until she opened her eyes and looked above them. She gasped.

"Look at all the stars!" She had never seen such a display—such brilliance in the sky. "There must be millions and millions of them!"

He followed her gaze, a flicker of a smile on his face. He returned his gaze to her. "Pricilla?"

"Yes, my love?"

He cinched her closer to him, his hands at her waist, warming her as the night cooled. "I want to spend the rest of my life solving the mystery of you. I love you."

And there, beneath a billion stars, Wade Prince dropped to his knees in the sand. "Will you marry me, Cilla?"

With no haze in the sky whatsoever, Priscilla shouted, "Yes!"

~

"You knew about this?"

Priscilla wrapped her arms around Amber, hugging her close. After Wade proposed, they had walked the beach for a long while, dreaming together about their future. So many plans—new home, family, friends all around her now—her heart was full. They'd arrived back at her condo, an engagement party waiting for them.

"No. I didn't find out about it until I was at Gwynnie's." She giggled. "Then we got to spy on you from inside the dunes."

"Really? You were spying on us?"

"Yeah, and we kept telling Sadie to shush." Amber looked at Priscilla's hands. "Good thing you got most of that paint off."

Priscilla held out her left hand, showing off the ring Wade had given her. It sparkled, but more than that, its uniqueness reflected his thoughtfulness. She never wanted to take it off, not even for a minute.

"It's one of the most beautiful rings I've ever seen," Liddy said, joining them.

Gwynnie padded across the living room from the kitchen where she'd been refilling appetizers. "My brother couldn't make up his mind! Until he did. And then there was no stopping him."

Meg stepped over, giving Priscilla a side hug. "I was honored to be there, but honestly, he didn't listen to me at all."

"Typical!" Gwynnie said.

"Whoa. Whoa. Ladies, are you mocking me?" Wade's glare was fake and they all knew it.

Meg winked. "We would never!"

Wade's gaze connected with Priscilla's and she shifted slightly, her hand still lingering on Amber's back.

He held his hand out to the teen. "Amber, may I speak to you?"

The young girl looked at Priscilla and frowned. "Go on," Priscilla whispered.

Wade took Amber's hand and led her to the couch. The entire room went quiet—not an easy feat for this crew.

He pulled a box from his pocket and opened it for Amber to see. The ring shone brilliantly even indoors. Her frown gradually began to change, her expression questioning. "This is for you," Wade said. "I love you, Amber, and can't wait for us all to be a family." He took the ring from the box. "May I?" Then he slid the delicate ring onto Amber's finger.

Priscilla sat next to him now, smiling big. "We would like to adopt you, honey."

Amber's eyes widened, fat tears filling them. Sobs followed and she lunged forward with a cry, landing squarely between them, knocking both Wade and Priscilla over until all three of them were overtaken by peals of laughter.

The partygoers sent up a cheer, followed by tears and hugs and more laughter than Priscilla's little condo had ever heard. Soon Amber was standing in the middle of them, showing off her ring to the oohs and aahs of the women in the room.

When no one appeared to be watching, Wade turned to Priscilla and kissed her hungrily.

A new kind of joy filled her, pouring over. "I always knew it," she said.

He raised a brow. "Knew what?"

She took in every beautiful inch of his face, her hand reaching up to trace the edges that had softened over time. She smiled, a giddiness overtaking her. "That someday ... my Prince would come."

<<<<>>>>

DEAR READER

Thank you for reading this fourth installment of the Sea Glass Inn novels! This series started with *Walking on Sea Glass* (book 1), which is loosely based on a true story (mine). I had only planned to write that one book, but my readers asked for more and I couldn't have been happier to keep writing.

Special shout-outs to Denise Harmer for editing help and Roseanna White for another gorgeous cover!

Big thanks to my husband, Dan, for inspiring this series, and our kids—Matt, Angie, Emma, and my parents, Dan and Elaine Navarro—for putting up with my angst while writing it.

Extra special thanks go to Emma for sharing your hair-styling expertise with me … and Priscilla :-).

If you enjoyed *Beneath a Billion Stars*, would you consider reviewing it at your favorite online retailer and/or Goodreads? Just a line or two would be so appreciated.

Thanks again,
Julie

ABOUT THE AUTHOR

JULIE CAROBINI writes inspirational beach romances and cozy mysteries ... with a twist. She is known for spunky heroines, charming heroes, quirky friends, and the secrets they keep. Her bestselling titles include *Walking on Sea Glass*, *Runaway Tide*, *Windswept*, the Otter Bay Novels, T*he Christmas Thief*, and more. Julie has received awards for writing and editing from The National League of American Pen Women and ACFW, and she is a double finalist for the ACFW Carol Award. She lives by the beach in California with her husband, Dan, and loves traveling and hanging out with her three 20-something kids. Grab a free eBook here: www.juliecarobini.com/free-book

Made in the USA
Monee, IL
11 May 2020